Fiona Tarr

Reign of Retribution

Book 3

The Eternal Realm

Copyright material ©

All rights reserve

Foreword

I am not in the habit of adding forewords to my books, but this story brought up a few details that could require a little clarification for my regular readers.

This book has a character called Jezebel and for those of you who have read my *Covenant of Grace* series, I thought it best to clarify any possible confusion up front. As I wave my Jedi hand through the air I utter the words *'she is not the Jezebel you are thinking of.'*

The Jezebel in *Reign of Retribution* is the real Biblical Jezebel. She inspired the Egyptian Jezebel in the *Covenant of Grace* series, but they are very different characters.

In the interests of keeping this book flowing well, I had to change the names of two main characters from the original Biblical story. So, for those who like to pick up the Bible and read the stories after reading my fictional versions, or to see how authentic, or how historically accurate or even theologically accurate I have been, I wanted to mention these two characters now.

Athaliah, whose name was simply too close to Ahaziah, her son's, has been changed to Thaliah.

The main character Jehosheba, whose name was also very close to another character's, has been changed to Sheba.

These changes have ensured that the flow of each scene is not interrupted by readers flicking through the historical Dynasty Chart (included at the back of this book) in a desperate effort to find out who is talking to whom.

Prologue

The prince opened his eyes to the sound of bells ringing in the night. The clash of iron on iron, men yelling, and painful cries set his heart racing as he sat up in bed. He held his breath as he tried to get his bearings in the darkness.

He rolled to the floor and crawled to the door of his room. With shaking hands, he opened the door a sliver. As he peaked out, he could see armed men moving through the hallway with lanterns aloft. He quickly closed the door as he realised they were not his father's guards.

On his hands and knees once more, he followed the floor rug to the door of his clothing cupboard. As he slid inside and closed the door, the crash of timber beyond invaded his senses and he stifled a scream.

He took a deep breath and turned to find the hidden panel he was looking for. He held his breath and slid the panel open, praying to whomever was listening for the men now inside his room not to hear him.

He reached for his scabbard before moving inside the passageway and slid the door in place. He had barely taken a step when the sound of men inside his robe closet filtered through the timber panelling. He stood motionless for a heartbeat before gently touching the wall and feeling his way.

The hidden passages were his playground and he knew them well. Even in pitch darkness, he was not about to get lost. His mind was reeling at what was happening within his father's palace. Who would invade the Kingdom of Judah and attack the King's home?

He came to the door he was looking for and touched his ear against the panel, listening for any sound from within. His heart raced in his ears, but he willed himself to remain calm.

He strapped on his scabbard before opening the door and slid out silently into the cook-house. He could hear screams coming from all directions and for a moment he was too frightened to move but the thought of his sister's safety kept him focussed.

All he had was his sword, but if there were a lot of soldiers, he knew he needed more. He moved toward the barracks to find a more substantial weapon. The barracks had been emptied out. The King's guards were lined up on their knees in the training yard, a group of enemy soldiers guarding them.

The Prince tried to distinguish the uniform in the darkness, but it was impossible. He shook his head to focus himself and moved into the armoury. He took a dagger and strapped it to his thigh, then collected a bow and a quiver of arrows.

He had to reach his sister and he knew he was running out of time. He moved past the harem and reached the women's apartments. Guards were pulling women and children from their beds in their nightgowns and the Prince watched, wondering how he was going to reach his sister.

'We have a lively one here.' A guard dragged a young woman from her room and the Prince had to force himself to stay calm. His sister, Sheba was on her knees, holding the hand of the guard who gripped a handful of her beautiful black hair.

'Take your hands off me. Now!' The Princess screamed as the guard took a tighter handful of her hair and yanked.

The guard dragged a dagger from his thigh scabbard and touched it to the Princess's throat. The Prince drew an arrow from his quiver and loaded the bow. He had little training with the weapon but to do nothing was not an option.

He drew the arm back and focussed his aim, waiting for the guard to stand up enough so that hitting Sheba was unlikely.

'What do you want here?' Sheba demanded, trying anything to delay her death.

'The end of your heathen line Princess.' The guard replied and his comrades chuckled as he drew his dagger back, ready to cut Sheba's throat. The Princess rolled sideways to avoid the blade as the guard's grip on her hair suddenly released.

She jumped from her knees to see an arrow protruding from his chest. She ran, not caring to see who was firing.

'Sheba.' The Prince jumped up and released the second arrow he had loaded while his sister had made her escape. It took another guard in the shoulder.

'Ahaziah! What is going on?' Sheba ran to the Prince and he grabbed her around the waist. He loaded another arrow as two guards followed the Princess.

One arrow took the guard on the left in the chest, but the other carried on undeterred.

'Let us get out of here.' Ahaziah coaxed and the Princess followed without a word.

They ran from the women's quarters into the shadows and held their breath as the remaining guard swore curses into the darkness. Ahaziah took Sheba's hand and they slid along the stone wall until they found the familiar tunnel that they knew would take them to safety.

Chapter 1

The soldier strutted into the grand hall as though he owned every stone he walked upon. His broad chest and tanned, muscular arms were hard to miss. Sheba cast her eyes down quickly. As she looked up again, trying carefully not to make eye contact with anyone, she found her brother, Ahaziah smiling good-naturedly in her direction.

He quickly regained his composure, straightened his royal robe and cast a quick eye toward his mother before nodding for the Priest to allow the King's man to address the court.

'The King will see you now.' Jehoiada waved his hand ceremoniously, bowing deeply but Sheba could not help but notice the lack of genuine respect in the priest's actions.

'Your Grace. Your Uncle, the King of Israel invites you to join him and your Grandmother, Jezebel at the fortress in Jezreel. He is resting there while he recovers from his most recent battle. He wishes to update you on the progress of the battle at Ramoth. However, he would like to debrief you and your generals in person.'

The soldier bowed but his eyes drifted from the King to take in the room and its surroundings.

The Queen-Mother snorted at the obvious directive in the invitation and scowled at her son.

Sheba saw none of the exchange. Instead, she caught the soldier's eye and recognition finally struck her. Her hand reached her mouth in time to stop the gasp, but the priest Jehoiada saw the Princess's reaction and frowned. She swallowed the lump in her throat and returned her eyes to the ground at her feet.

'Is he doing well?' Sheba was drawn back into the formalities. The Queen-Mother's question held no emotion and the Princess watched her stepmother closely as she waited for an answer.

The woman saw Sheba staring at her and her eyes drifted from the Princess to the Priest. A smirk crept across her face. The gesture made the Princess feel uncomfortable, but she forced herself to focus on their visitor.

'He is recovering from some minor injuries my lady. Rest assured, he will be fighting fit by the time your son meets with him.' The soldier watched the gathered court with wary eyes and Sheba smiled as memories she had all but forgotten came drifting in on the cool breeze that swept through the court.

The soldier looked to the young Princess and a smile turned the corner of his lips as he realised she remembered him. The hair on the back of his neck stood on end as the breeze reached him and he shivered slightly.

Sheba watched Aron shiver and like a cascading waterfall, felt the chill of cold water run down her own back.

****

'I do not like it Ahaziah. My brother is up to something. The Queen-Mother paced restlessly.

'I'm sure Jehoram means no ill will to me. I would be more worried about the zealot factions than my own uncle.'

'My mother is the cause of all this.' Thaliah sighed with frustration.

'Jezebel! Why on earth would you say that? Grandmother is an amazing woman.' The King took a seat and put his feet up on the long table in his private chambers.

'You still see with the eyes of a child. Grow up Ahaziah.' His mother pushed his feet to the floor, almost unbalancing the King.

The King sniffed loudly and choked back a laugh. 'Anyone would think *you* were still the Queen.'

'No offence child but it took my extraordinary talent to look after *your* Kingdom while you decided to grow up. When your father died, there was no shortage of pressure for me to re-marry, but I had no intention of letting anyone outside of our family rule in this place.' She poured a goblet of watered wine and took a seat at the King's table.

'All lines come to an end eventually Mother.'

'Not this one. Not while I still draw breath.' Thaliah pointed her finger at her son. 'I have made sacrifices to the gods to ensure our line reigns over all of Israel.'

'Which gods? What sacrifices?' Ahaziah laughed good-naturedly but as he watched his mother's eyes he knew he had once more pushed her too far. 'Relax Mother. I was jesting.'

'As I said.' Thaliah took a deep breath to compose herself. 'My Mother is the cause of all of this. Elijah was an influential prophet. It was he who foretold how important our line could be.

It was a mistake for her to encourage the worship of Baal, Asherah and all the gods of the enemies of Israel and Judah so openly, but killing the priests,' Thaliah shook her head, 'killing them only served to put a target on our entire family's back.' She gulped down her wine and began to pour another.

'I thought you supported the gods of the common people?' The young King frowned in confusion. 'I have never agreed with the teachings of Baal myself, nor does your brother, but you have been to the temple many times.'

'Of course I visit the Temple. I have allies everywhere.' She stopped pouring and thumped the jug down on the table irritably.

'You mean we?' Thaliah looked deeply into her son's eyes and vaguely realised he was challenging her with his question.

'Yes darling. *Our* allies.' She smiled but it failed to reach her eyes. 'You are my pride and joy, you know that? You are all I have left. Your father was an idiot. He publicly renounced the Israelite God and our entire family paid the price. You have brought a son to the line and the gods have promised me the Kingdom.' She swung her arm in the air theatrically.

'Leave Joash out of this Mother. He is not even one year old.' Ahaziah watched as his Mother's eyes glazed over. 'I think you might have had too much wine Mother.'

'I do not need to be managed by you, child.'

'I am not a child Mother. I am the King.'

'Do not forget who put you there.' Thaliah stood and moved from the table. Her chair nearly toppled to the ground, but she steadied it with her hand. With unnecessary effort, she swished her long robe before pulling it closely around her body. She spun toward the door to leave, but stopped momentarily. 'This audience is over.'

Ahaziah shook his head as he watched his Mother leave his private meeting chambers, slamming the large wooden door in her wake.

Sheba snuck out from her hiding place and sighed quietly as she approached the tall backed chair that sat at the head of the long, wide, heavy wooden table. Her brother was slumped over, with his head held in his hands and she could not help but wonder how he remained so calm with his Mother.

She patted his back gently. 'Are you going to see Uncle?' Her words were soft and quiet.

Ahaziah lifted his head. He rubbed his eyes, the weariness evident now that the Princess was close to him. 'It was not an invitation; it was a command. You heard it.'

'I can talk with Aron. Find out what he knows.'

'Who is Aron?' The King frowned, as he motioned for Sheba to take a seat.

'The soldier. Did you not recognise him?' The Princess smoothed her dress as she sat.

'I saw you blush when he walked in. A handsome fellow for sure,' Ahaziah grinned, 'but why should I remember him?'

'Father appointed a bodyguard to look after me, before the attack that….'

'That killed everyone. Mother never lets me forget. She is still angry that I helped you escape and did not look for her.'

'I am sorry Ahaziah. It was not your fault. You did what you thought was right and I am so glad you did. It was not father's fault either. He never publicly denounced Yahweh.' Sheba forced herself to stay on task, physically shaking her head to return to the present.

'Aron was not only my bodyguard, he trained me. Your mother does not know, so please never say a word, but father was worried about the Queen.'

'I know she has been ill, but what did father say to you? Why could he not tell me?'

'Because she is your Mother and you are her son Ahaziah. She has never really liked me. In fact, if you leave, I am certain she is going to marry me off to the old Priest.'

Ahaziah laughed aloud, the sound deep and full of emotion. 'She hardly notices anyone but herself Sheba and the Priest is not old. He is not even in his thirtieth year.'

'She wants allies and what better ally than a man of the temple? You know how much the Zealots hate our family for not killing everyone who worships Baal. Uncle still turns a blind eye.'

'Uncle honours Yahweh, so do I. We just do not believe we have the right to choose a god for all the people. If Yahweh wants everyone to follow Him, He is big enough and strong enough to make Himself known to them all.'

'You know the Zealots say that is what He does through the religious wars against the Moabites, the Amorites and all *their gods*'.

'A God that can feed the starving with bread from the desert does not need an army to fight his battles Sheba.'

'So very wise for one so young. That may be the case but your Mother does not believe the same as you and she wants to marry me off to that old Priest.' The Princess changed the subject. 'I am telling you. I saw it in her eyes today. It makes my blood run cold.'

'I will tell her you are not her ward to promise to anyone and if she does so without my permission, she will answer to me.'

Sheba giggled and Ahaziah leant forward and hugged her as they both continued to laugh her fears away.

'So, you are trained to fight? Father was always a clever man.'

'Aron was young when he was given the role to guard me. He was still well trained, having grown up in the army. We grew very close.'

'How close?'

'Close enough for Father to send him away to serve his brother-in-law in Israel.

Chapter 2

Jehoiada drew his ornate robes up around his cheeks as he left the palace. The sun had dipped quickly from the horizon and the night air was growing crisper by the second.

He mulled over his conversation with the Queen-Mother again. He felt as though he were making a deal with the beast below himself, but he needed access to the Prince. Joash was the future. He needed to be schooled in the ways of Yahweh. Foreign gods were not to be permitted.

When Thaliah had offered to make him a part of the King's court, it had been too great an opportunity, but now he felt the pressure of his decision.

The Queen-Mother was unstable. She worshipped Baal even if she claimed she did not. She spent too many hours visiting her *allies* in the chambers of the temple of Baal and now there was talk of other heathen gods being served through sacrifice.

He had been so close to telling the King what he knew but then Thaliah had offered him the Princess in marriage. Sheba was a beautiful young woman and it was a great honour to be betrothed to a Princess. His own future line would be linked to the great kings of old.

The mere thought gave him goosebumps, but they were nothing compared to the dreams he was now having of Sheba's soft bronze skin and deep brown eyes.

It was written that Yahweh had said that a Priest could serve Yahweh best unmarried and Jehoiada had kept that vow for many years, but Samuel had a wife, had he not? Why should he not feel the pleasures of the flesh? King David himself had so many wives.

Jehoiada shook his head at his own day dreaming. If he were one of his altar boys he would have slapped himself in the head to draw himself back on task.

The Priest rounded the side of the temple and began his descent to the lower floor and his private chambers below the vestibule.

'Nice of you to finally join us Jehoiada.' The Priest nearly left his sandals at the door as he jumped back from the deep, commanding voice that filled his chest and made his heart skip a beat.

'Jehu! What are you doing here?' He took a deep breath to calm himself.

'Jehoram failed at Ramoth.' The general stood with his hands folded across his chest.

His tone indicated his statement had answered all the Priest's questions.

'Interesting, but that does not answer my question.' Jehoiada's fear had now subsided and was being replaced with indignation. 'You enter the place where only the ordained can enter.'

'I *am* ordained, *called* to be here. That is likely more than I can say for you Priest.'

'Called? What on earth are you talking about? I have seen no prophecy.'

'You are a Priest, not a Prophet. Elisha has anointed me the next King of Israel.' Jehu puffed out his chest, giving him a fearsome appearance in the low lantern light.

Jehoiada paused a moment, trying desperately to compose himself. 'You have some official documentation?' He was surprised at how smooth his own voice sounded.

'Of course.' The General reached into his tunic pocket and drew out a worn parchment. 'Scribed by Elisha's own hand.'

Jehoiada reached for the document and held it in his hand. The General did not release it immediately. 'Where is the King?' the Priest asked, feeling unusually brave.

'In Jezreel. You have heard the invitation?'

'I did. I was just not sure that it was accurate. What are your plans?'

'None of your concern Priest.' The General released the parchment. 'Your work will come after the Judah throne is left vacant.'

The Priest paused a moment as he digested the General's words. 'You are the King's man. What are you planning?' His forehead creased; his palms grew sweaty.

'As I said, none of your business. Are you going to read that decree?' The General nodded to the parchment, now forgotten in Jehoiada's hand.

'You cannot possibly do what I think you are planning to do.' The Priest focussed on the matter at hand.

'I am *called*.' Jehu pouted, nodding to the still unread document. 'I will take the Kingdom. Elisha has spoken. Read the letter.'

'David was called, but he did not kill Saul.' The priest shook the unopened, still furled parchment in his fist.

'Do not presume to lecture me Priest. Elisha has anointed me. Yahweh is with me.' Jehu snarled and moved toward Jehoiada, who took a step backward, maintaining the space between them.

'Yes, you said that. But there is a reason Elijah never acted against this Kingdom—a reason that Elisha seems to have forgotten. His mentor knew that this line is the line of King David. It must continue!'

Jehu moved so fast he nearly knocked Jehoiada from his feet. He clutched the fine priestly robes in his fist. His hot breath fell upon the man's face as he tried unsuccessfully not to shiver. 'Ahaziah has a son. Young enough to be schooled. You will ensure he survives Priest.'

'Why would he not? Are you attacking the palace, right here?'

'Of course not. The Kings will both die in Jezeel but sometimes matters do not always go to plan. Elisha and I have discussed this at length. The Prophet will make his way here to speak with the Queen-Mother once I am named King in Israel.

'What then?' Jehoiada could feel the sweat running down his back.

'Then we will appoint a new Regent over Judah, one who cleanses the Kingdom of all those who worship the false gods. Every Baal temple, every forest with Asherah idols, everything will burn and our Lord will reign once more.'

****

Jehu left the temple on foot and made his way to the stables under the cover of darkness.

He and his small group of soldiers quietly prepared their mounts, ready to leave before first light.

Aron watched the General leave before heading back to the Palace and Sheba. He had tracked Jehu from the temple to the stables and was now even more concerned than he had been before.

Sheba had left the gate to the garden unlocked and Aron made his way into the palace garden.

****

Sheba threw the dark purple hood over her head and wrapped the long lightly woven woollen robe tightly around her shoulders, more for courage than warmth. She moved in the shadows to ensure she would not be seen.

The pool of water shone in the moonlight and the sound of the cicada hung in the cool evening air. Summer was fading and with it the comforting, familiar sound would be gone once more.

The trees swayed in the breeze, rustling loud enough to cover her movements. Sheba pulled back her hood as she reached her rendezvous.

'I wondered if you would come.' The voice was soft, yet deep, sending tingles throughout the Princess's body.

'Nothing would keep me away.' She moved toward the voice in the darkness below a tall, bowing palm tree.

'You have changed.' Aron moved to greet the Princess who fell into his embrace.

'So have you.' Sheba could feel Aron's strength and for the first time since her father passed, since Aron was sent away, she felt safe and secure.

Aron took Sheba's shoulders in his hands and held her at arm's length. 'You are more beautiful than I remember.'

The Princess cast her eyes down, thankful that the night covered her blushing cheeks.

'Do not hide Sheba.' Aron lifted her chin, trying to make eye contact in the dimness of the night. 'You are stronger than you think.'

The Princess took his hand and led him deeper into the garden. She sat on a hard-stone bench amongst thick, manicured hedges of climbing jasmine and pulled him to sit beside her.

'A lot has happened since you left Aron.'

'I never left Sheba. I was sent away. You know I would never have gone willingly.' He took both her hands in his.

'I know, but our family is in tatters now. Father is gone, most of our brothers and sisters are dead. Even Ahaziah lost the mother of his son in child birth.'

'Lucky you have so many nephews and nieces.' Sheba could hear the mirth in Aron's voice. 'How many wives has Ahaziah taken?'

'He has never married. Zabiah and he were never wed. She was not worthy according to Thaliah. Instead, his mother filled his harem so that he would produce many sons but he has only fathered girls until Joash, Zabiah's only child.'

'Ahaziah and his heir are why I am here. Your Uncle could have sent anyone but he chose me because he knew you would listen to me.' Aron's tone was suddenly urgent.

'Ahaziah is in great danger. Jehoram did not call him to Jezeel lightly. The Zealots wish to bring war to Israel and Judah. They stir up mistrust with the temple of Baal and Asherah. Your Grandmother is furious.'

'I would love to see that.' Sheba smiled, but it was lost in the darkness.

'Jezebel and your uncle sent me to guard you once more.'

'What is it with Queen-Mothers and their meddling ways?'

'Jezebel is not Thaliah. They are different. She told me to tell you that Yahweh does not hate Asherah, or Baal or any of them; that it is the tiny minds of humanity. They have to box the gods into corners so they can make sense of them.'

'Why are you telling me this?' Aron was gently squeezing her hands now.

'Because she asked me to—because she said it was important that you understand the complexity of the gods and that protecting you, is paramount.'

'Why me? I am nothing—a token to be married off in the next politically viable transaction. The only reason I am eighteen and still unmarried is because I am all that is left, Ahaziah's only family.'

Aron ran his hands along the Princess's shoulders, but she shook them away. He knew she did not mean it. He knew she could defend herself if she truly wanted him to leave her alone. Instead he waited, knowing she would make the first move.

'I have missed you Aron.' She moved back into his embrace.

'I have missed you too Sheba.'

Chapter 3

The Goddess floated above the garden and watched over the young Princess. The moon was high and the silver streaks it cast on the dark night sky made Asherah think of home. She longed to stop, to rest, to leave humanity in peace. But peace was still a long way away and the Redeemer would never come if Moloch and his followers were left to wreak havoc.

'Why do you allow him to meddle Father and then say I should not?' The question was rhetorical. The Goddess knew her Father seldom spoke to His children with words. That is why she followed her heart. That is why she continued to do what she could to protect the Redeemer's line.

Asherah had watched Jezebel send the young soldier to protect her granddaughter. She had shared the vison of what was to come with the once Queen, hoping she would act.

'You hope to redeem Jezebel through this action?' Asherah spun around to see Moloch. Like her, he could change his appearance and today he wore a light tunic of leather with his bronze chest and muscular stomach exposed for all to see. She did not need to recognise his appearance to know who it was. His soul would never change. The scent of darkness drifted on the cool night air.

'Jezebel does not need my help to be redeemed. Father does not measure humanity's worth in deeds.'

'Here we go. Another of your misguided theologies.'

'It is you who is misguided Moloch. There is no black and white in Father's eyes. We, they,' Asherah cast her arm across the scene below and beyond. 'are all shades of grey to Him.'

'So, there is no good or evil?' Moloch laughed aloud knowing only Asherah could hear him.

'There is no good or evil brother. Look at what Father did for Dagon. No darker deeds had I seen and yet he found a place for him amongst the heavens.'

'Finally. You and I may have finally found common ground.'

'No Moloch. I understand now that good and evil are mute, but there is still right and wrong. You want humanity to attack itself, to bring about their own extinction. I want them to survive. I guarantee Father does to.'

'How can you be so sure! Father let the fallen loose upon the earth.'

'Yes, and you aid the fallen as we speak.'

'I do not aid the fallen. I feed humanity with what they want. I am not responsible for the choices they make. Father gave them choice, this is on Him, not me.'

'So you have issues with Father and you take them out on the innocent world below? You have lived for centuries and still you have not grown up. You are just a spoilt brat.'

'We can sling insults all night Asherah. You too have lived for centuries and you still think you can control all this?' Moloch shook his head and disappeared.

'Someone has to do something brother. To stand by and do nothing cannot be right.' Asherah watched Aron embrace the Princess and a sad smile drifted across her lips. 'I am so sorry child but not everyone finds happiness in this life.' The air rippled and a mist of silver streaked across the sky as the Goddess took flight.

****

Elisha read the well-worn parchment in his hand and took a deep breath. He hoped that reading his mentor's words once more would alleviate his feelings of inadequacy.

My disciple. I know that if you are reading these words, my time on this earth has passed and I am with the Father, walking the halls of Heaven.

I had hoped to spend more time with you. Your love of Yahweh is strong but I still had so much more I wished to teach you. Beware the teachings of man, for they are fraught with bias, opinion and motive. Look to the teachings of the Prophets who have come before. Look to the honourable figures of the Lord and follow their example.

Some will say, follow your heart for Yahweh is with you, but your heart can be deceived... so too can your ego, that is young and yet to mature in the spirit of Yahweh.

Be careful my son, but always remember, even if you make mistakes, know that in all things Yahweh works for the good of those who love him.

Not for the first time, Elisha wondered if this was the right and just course of action, but Elijah's last words were his saving grace. Even if he was making a mistake, everything would still be alright. Yet he could not push the feelings of doubt aside.

As he thought of the heroes of the past, he was reminded of King David, of how he did not dishonour himself by taking Saul's life, even when he could.

This was different. Saul was not worshipping false gods. Saul was not allowing the religions of others to thrive. No! This was different. Elisha felt a cold breeze enter the prayer room and he wrapped his robe tightly around his body.

He looked around the room, seeking the source, but there were no open windows, the door was closed. He shivered again and looked above him at the heavy thatch ceiling. The sense of being watched washed over him, but it was not the kind of warm, blessed sense of peace he had hoped for.

****

'I have to admit brother, convincing one of Father's own Prophets to do our work for us is genius, but please tell me again how killing my followers will serve us?'

'Baal, you can be quite dense at times.' Moloch showed no humour in his words and Baal drew a deep breath. 'Calm down brother. For a dark lord, you can be a little sensitive you know.' This time he smiled to soften his words.

'I have worked hard to establish my minions. Killing them off is not part of my plan.'

'These worshippers are not the kind of followers you want Baal. They think for themselves. Jezebel has never truly been your follower. Have you ever really listened to her thoughts?'

Baal looked at Moloch as though he had grown another pair of horns. The crease between his heavy loose-skinned brow furrowed even further and the ceremonial ring he wore in his nose twitched with his concentration.

'Cannot say that I have.'

'Have you noticed she also worships Asherah? Now you and our sister could not be further apart in ethos, but does Jezebel know? Of course not.'

'Now you are just talking gibberish to me brother. If you think this is the right course of action, then I am with you. You have never led me astray before. Dagon on the other hand. I think you might have played our poor brother in that Delilah debacle.'

Moloch shrugged. 'He had my full support until he attacked our sisters. The whole point to me Baal is to restore *us*, not the feeble humans to power in Father's Kingdom. Dagon strayed from the path.'

'Remind me to never piss you off brother.'

Moloch's grin was mischievous but there was malice not missed by Baal. 'Do not forget it brother. Not even for the blink of an eye.'

Chapter 4

Sheba had left the gate to the garden unlocked once more. Aron entered quietly and made his way past the harem, past the women's and children's wing of the Palace, toward the Princess's room. It was like his feet were working on their own, for he had walked this path a hundred times when he would guard and train the Princess.

Her father, King Jerom was a wise man. He had known that his open acceptance of the common people following their ancient gods would end in pain.

Aron had asked him once why he allowed the worship of other gods if he knew it was going to cause political unrest. The King's answer had been inspiring. *You will understand one day boy that sometimes you must do the right thing, even when it could cause you or those you love pain.*

Right now, he truly understood those words. He only hoped Sheba would forgive him when the time came.

She had left a candle burning in the window as they had agreed. He took a deep breath to calm himself. The sight of her had come as a shock to him. He knew his heart had been hers for years, but he had not expected it to feel like it was going to explode into tiny pieces the moment he saw her again.

He knocked gently on the door. The curtain flickered at the window as she checked to see it was him before opening the door a crack. 'Just as I trained you. Nice to know you were paying attention.'

He squeezed through the small opening as she stepped back just long enough to allow him entry.

'You will be surprised what I have learnt in your absence.' She closed the door behind her, guarding it as though she thought he might escape.

'You look like you are preparing to attack.' Aron smiled at her posture. Her confidence was growing so quickly.

'I am.' Sheba moved forward and Aron put his hand up gently, realising her intent.

'We cannot do this Sheba. You are the last Princess of your Father's line.'

'Do what?' Sheba moved Aron's hand aside and pushed him slowly toward the chair that sat alongside her four-posted bed. Aron sat as soon as his legs touched the hard wood and the Princess hitched up her skirt and sat on his lap, one leg either side. 'I was only going to kiss you.' Her lips devoured his and the young soldier fought her for only a heartbeat. Moments passed before he came to his senses, but it was too late. She knew she had had the desired effect.

'We cannot. Every bone in my body wants you. You know it does but I am a soldier and you are a Princess. You will be married to someone noble, someone of worth.'

Sheba pushed herself to her feet. She knew he was right and she knew she should not be angry with him, but she was. 'And you will just stand by and let it happen.'

'I am not leaving you shamed and unable to marry honourably. Your father would turn over in his grave. You had forgotten all about me until yesterday. You will forget again.'

'I had not and I will not and what do you mean *leaving me*?' Aron's words had sunk in, past her rising emotions and her heart suddenly ached as though she had been punched in the chest.

Aron stood from the chair and gently guided Sheba to take the seat. He sat next to her on the white and purple covered soft linen bedspread and held her hand. He stroked the inside of her palm as he spoke, her eyes fixed on his as he watched her delicate fingers, avoiding her intense gaze.

'War is coming to us all Sheba. The Zealots are planning something. Ahaziah needs to know it. I must meet with him again… privately. Without your Stepmother. Can you arrange it?'

'Of course, but that does not explain why you believe you will need to leave me. You are staying here, right?'

'Yes I am. But if the vision your Grandmother had is true, war is coming here too. She sent me to guard you Sheba. You!'

'That still does not explain you leaving. In fact, you have not explained Jezebel's vision much at all. What else did she see?'

'Nothing. Nothing that matters right now. I will explain soon, I just need to do some investigating before I see your brother. I have to go now!'

'Go where?'

'Best you do not know, that way if you are asked, you can answer truthfully.' Aron smiled and leant over, softly placing a kiss on the Princess's forehead.

'No, you do not get away that easily.' Sheba pulled his face to her lips with both hands so quickly and strongly that Aron did not have time to resist. 'No-one was shunned from marriage because of a few passionate kisses. You are mine Aron. You understand me.'

The young soldier smiled between kisses and her breathy words before he rose to leave. 'I always was my lady.' Aron bowed and stepped back. 'I will be back in the garden tomorrow night. Can you have our meeting arranged by then?'

Sheba nodded as Aron stepped forward, took her hand and kissed it, then he turned and left.

The Princess felt numb inside and out. What in heaven's name just happened? One moment she was ready to give herself to a man without any sense of propriety and the next she was watching him leave. Again!

What was he not telling her? Being the youngest daughter of a King to his concubine was probably worse than being a peasant. Well at least that is how it felt right now. At least a peasant could rut with whomever she wanted to.

Chapter 5

'Mother, please stop pacing. That is an order.' Jezebel looked at her son, ready to rebuke him when she saw the concern in Jehoram's eyes.

'I cannot sit Jehoram. The damned Zealots have been looking to end me from the moment I arrived in Israel.'

'Then why are you so anxious this time?'

'Because! Just because.' Jezebel could not bring herself to share the vision the Goddess had bestowed upon her. In truth, she wished the deity had kept it to herself.

The Queen-Mother flopped upon a bright blue divan and sighed. 'Wine! Bring me wine!' A servant jumped to attention and ran from the marble floored courtyard. Jezebel sighed again as she took a deep breath, trying to absorb the serenity of the creeping vines and scented flowers that clung to the tall stone walls around her.

'You will be safe here Mother. I will meet Jehu and his wayward faction when the time comes.'

'You are in no fit state to meet anyone. Look at you. That wound in your shoulder still seeps blood.' Jezebel rose from her seat, collecting a shawl from the back of the divan as she went. 'We need to call the physician again.' She leant over her son, pushing the shawl inside his tunic and began tearing the ends with her teeth, making ties to hold it in place.

'Stop fussing Mother. We knew it was only a matter of time before the followers of Yahweh sought retribution.' The King adjusted his position, trying to get comfortable.

'Retribution for what? I was an orphan of my own people, flung into a strange place with a man I did not know. Do not get me wrong. I loved your father—in my own way.'

'You do not have to recount the story Mother; it is known by all.' Jehoram touched his Mother's tending hands gently. His soft eyes pleaded with her to stop tormenting herself. 'I know you were young and frightened. It must have been a nightmare leaving everything you had known behind!'

'You have no idea my son. If not for the Goddess, I would have killed myself.'

'The Goddess?' Jehoram pushed himself more upright in his seat. He had never heard his mother speak openly of the Goddess.

'Asherah. She has stayed with me throughout these years. When your father built the monument to Baal, he was only trying to make me feel at home. I used to help my father in the temple of Asherah and I was so afraid when I first arrived.'

'But father began to follow Baal?' Jehoram raised a questioning eyebrow. He was the only one of his family with pale grey eyes and Jezebel smiled as his beautiful soul shone through them.

'No.' She shook her head. 'But that is what the Zealots thought and it did not take long for them to start horrid rumours about your father and I. They would do anything to keep their people in check—under their control. All I ever wanted to do was be accepted here. But the indoctrinated cast of old men was never going to allow that.'

'Mother, you did kill at least a hundred of their brethren.'

'It was self-defence.' Jehoram looked into his mother's almost black eyes and paused. For a moment, she was that little Princess, bargained to bed a King for trade routes to the sea. 'Asherah was angry with me when I did it. But they deserved it.' Jezebel pouted to make her point.

'What is done is done Mother. No-one blames you.' Jehoram looked up and patted her hand, still on his wounded shoulder.

'Yes, they do blame me, but that is not the point. I was a child. I was angry and frightened and I lashed out. Then Elijah killed all my friends and I was alone again.'

'Sit mother! Please!' Jehoram patted the sun coloured cushion next to him and coaxed his mother to join him. He embraced her and stroked her hair as he had seen his father do so many times before.

'Why did you send Thaliah to Judah, knowing how you felt when you were young?'

Jezebel pulled back to look her son squarely in the eye. 'You think we had a choice? Women never have a choice Jehoram. Just remember that when you bargain your daughters into marriage.'

Chapter 6

Aron watched the service. It had been many years since he had graced the threshold of the temple courtyard. It was not that he did not believe. In fact, it was entirely the opposite. He believed with all his heart. He would not be here if he did not. It was the institute that he did not believe in. Corruption was rife as it was in all circles of power and the followers of Yahweh were no different.

Jehoiada finished the service with a final prayer and left the temple steps waving an incense cup, leaving a waft of sandalwood in his wake as he entered the vestibule of the holy place within.

Aron waited for the courtyard to empty out, knowing that the Priest would be within, clearing away the ceremonial instruments in case of theft.

He entered the vestibule and stopped to take in the holy place where only the priests were permitted. The ceiling was high, with a stone altar in the central hall. Beyond, two large statues guarded the sacred ark within.

He saw the priest, tidying objects around the menorah which sat upon the altar. His heart was breaking with every moment that ticked by. He knew what he had to do. Jezebel had been adamant in her interpretation of the vision, but was it right? Surely visions were subjective.

The priest removed his scarlet, blue and purple tunic, folding it so the onyx stones and gold chain were on top. Without his High Priest garments, he appeared less imposing—just a tall, lean man with a long beard and eyes hidden below bushy brown eyebrows.

'May I have a word?' Aron approached the altar, but did not stand upon the raised steps surrounding it.

Jehoiada jumped but quickly regained his composure as he recognised the soldier. Then he suddenly felt uncomfortable, wondering why the young man was there.

'I am afraid I am at a loss young man. How should I address you?'

'Aron, my name is Aron.'

'What can I do for you Aron? The service is over and you are not permitted inside the vestibule uninvited.'

'I apologise for the intrusion, but I am here to speak with you. I have a few questions.'

'Do you ask on behalf of the King?' He sniffed, raising his nose in the air as if to reiterate that Aron was uninvited.

'No. I ask on behalf of the Princess!'

Jehoiada remained silent a moment, once more wondering what the soldier knew. He decided to tread carefully. Aron could not possibly know of his arrangement with the Queen-Mother.

'What does the Princess wish to know?' He kept his tone mildly curious.

'She does not know I am here.' Aron watched the priest carefully. He seemed casual enough, but there was something in his manner that seemed uncomfortable.

'Speak plainly boy. I do not have all day.' The Priest continued tidying up the altar and was preparing to return to his rooms when Aron spoke into the silence.

'Plainly you say. Alright. Why do you conspire with General Jehu?'

Jehoiada stopped his fussing and cautiously turned to look at Aron. The soldier had not drawn a weapon. He simply looked accusingly into the Priest's eyes for answers.

'I do not understand the question.' Jehoiada averted his gaze.

'There is no point hedging around the truth Priest. Even if you lie to me, Yahweh will know the truth of your words.'

'Do not think to lecture me boy. I am a High Priest, a man of the temple and you are, you are, a nobody.'

'Yes, so was King David, a nobody that is. Your unwillingness to cooperate is answer enough. I have seen you with Jedu. Just know that you will have to choose sides eventually and if you choose wrongly, you will lose Sheba along with everything else you hold dear.'

The Priest was speechless. How could he know about his bargain with the Queen-Mother? 'Who are you?'

'Just a nobody Priest, just a nobody.' Aron turned on his heel and headed for the tall columns that would lead to the courtyard beyond the temple.

'Wait! Please wait!'

Aron did not turn around. He could see the Priest was not a leader. He was anybody's to manipulate. Now he had to convince Sheba she needed to manipulate him or die.

Chapter 7

Thaliah pushed her way past the acolyte guarding the door. He attempted to stop her, but one scathing look was all it took to change his mind. She made her way to the stone altar at the rear of the building. Ignoring all convention, she lifted her long blue silk robe and stepped up onto the stained grey stone steps and approached the sacrificial slab. 'Mattan!'

'Thaliah. So very lovely to see you again.' The Priest casually rose from his kneeling position and turned to face the Queen-Mother.

'Do not be smart with me Mattan.'

'Of course not. I was merely being polite. It is not customary to have anyone approach the altar of Baal uninvited. I thought I was being more than accommodating.'

Thaliah looked closely at the Priest. There was something strange about his eyes, an intensity she tried not to flinch away from. He was usually more easily intimidated and his manner bordered on haughty.

'You have news?' Mattan smiled and Thaliah focussed on her reason for coming.

'Yes. You have my tonic?' Thaliah looked expectantly at the Priest who smiled.

'Of course. Your news first.' Mattan indicated for her to follow him as he stepped down from the altar.

The Queen-Mother took a deep breath. 'Ahaziah has been summoned to join my brother in Jezeel.'

'And?' Thaliah stared daggers at the Priest's back as she followed him to the main temple floor.

'And you promised me the Kingdom. I want Ahaziah to have my brother's throne and I will take Judah for myself.' Mattan stopped and turned to face the Queen-Mother.

'Ah. I see. Your ambitions have grown since we bartered our deal.' The Priest turned to move away, but Thaliah grabbed his arm.

'Where do you think you are going?' Mattan stopped perfectly still and Thaliah felt a cold shudder run through her arm and into her body. She slowly released the hand that held the Priest and tried not to rub the numbness away.

'I was going to get your tonic.'

'What about my request?' Thaliah's voice was barely a whisper.

'Baal will consider your request I am sure, but how far are you willing to go to have the power you desire?'

Thaliah thought for a moment. She had enjoyed the power after her husband had died and her son had been too young to rule. *What was she willing to do to have it once more?*

'Short of killing my own son, I would do anything to regain my power.' She heard the words leave her lips and, in that moment, she knew they were true.

Mattan collected a dark blue vial from a side table and handed it to the Queen-Mother, placing it in her hand. He held it there with both of his own and smiled his understanding. Thaliah pulled her hand from his grasp and tried unsuccessfully to walk calmly from the temple.

The laughter that followed her was eerie and left a heavy feeling in her chest, causing her to take a deep, deliberate breath. She forced the tightness away as she pushed the laughter from her mind. Instead she found an alleyway with little or no traffic and pulled the cork on the pretty blue bottle. She drank the contents down in one mouthful.

****

'What did you give her, brother?' Mattan turned toward the voice. He waved his hand over his head and the image of the Priest disappeared, replaced with the bronze chested, golden haired Moloch.

'Just a narcotic. Something to soften her memory a little.'

'She could do with more than a little softening, of that there is no doubt. Will she kill the line when the time comes?'

'Do not fret Baal. She would kill her own son if we take away the narcotic long enough, but if the Zealots do what they plan, she will not need any encouragement. That woman wants power more than she craves air to breathe.'

Baal laughed and his nose ring rattled as his head and chest moved.

'You really should get rid of that ring. It makes you look more like a common bull than a minotaur.'

Baal touched his nose and frowned. 'I have been considering an image change. The peasants have taken to the carving in stone. It might be time for a more divine-like figure.'

Baal's body shimmered and grew taller. His big floppy ears receded, leaving a circlet of gold around an almost human looking head. His chest was bare to the waist where a heavy golden belt framed ornately carved strips of bronze to guard his thighs. His shins were covered in ivory inlaid shields and his feet were wrapped in leather sandals.

'I approve.' Moloch put his hands on his hips and nodded. 'Much more suited to a god.'

Chapter 8

Aron had spent most of the afternoon preparing his plan but now as he watched Sheba picking flowers in the royal gardens, his courage waned.

He had entered through the unlocked gate as before, but it was not yet nightfall and he was unsure if Sheba had made the necessary arrangements to meet with the King.

The Princess moved from the garden and made her way to a stone lounge, covered in brightly covered cushions. She placed her cut flowers on the ground and laid out on the divan to rest.

A servant saw her sit down and came to her side, a platter of food and refreshments in hand. He placed the food on the low table at the Princess's feet, collected her cut flowers and moved back toward the main building.

Aron knew the servant would keep watch, so he lowered himself to the ground, content to wait for nightfall.

'You had best come and eat something before we meet with my brother. You must be famished by now.'

Aron jumped at the sound of Sheba's voice and smiled as he rose from his hiding place behind a low hedge.

'How long have you known I was there?' he asked as he moved closer to the Princess.

'Since before I left the flower beds. You are quiet enough, but I think you need to take a bath if you expect to remain hidden in a garden of beautiful scents.'

Aron laughed. 'That bad?' He took a seat a good distance away, still smiling.

'Pretty bad.' The Princess screwed up her nose.

'Do I have time to clean up before Ahaziah meets with us?'

'I have already made arrangements.'

'What about Thaliah?'

'You are here as my guest. An old friend of my father's. She has little interest in anything to do with father.' Sheba picked a handful of nuts and seeds from the platter and put them in her mouth, one at a time.

'We need to keep her away when we meet with Ahaziah.'

'She has returned from the temple of Baal. She should be no trouble until at least later this evening.'

'Why is that?'

'She is an unstable woman. When Ahaziah came of age, it was a godsend. Now, the Queen-Mother is a little erratic to say the least. She is supposed to take herbs to calm her moods, but she drinks too much and has found another kind of *herb* in the temple of Baal. When she visits the temple, my brother thinks it is for political reasons, but when she returns, she is unconscious for most of the day.'

'That is unfortunate for her but fortuitous for us.' Aron grinned.

'It is, in a way. Let us get you cleaned up.' The Princess stood up and Aron jumped up reflexively.

'Us! I do not think so Princess. You point me in the right direction and I will see you back here when I am done.'

Sheba grinned and Aron felt his blood heating up. 'But I am very good with scented oils and hot water you know.'

'I have no doubt, but we have already had this conversation.'

The Princess pouted as she waved a hand to call her servant over, before sitting back down heavily on her cushions. 'Have it your way then. I will not offer again.'

'Yes, you will, but I will continue to keep my word Sheba. As hard as it is.'

The servant bowed, missing the Princess's wide smile. As he looked up, she wiped it away quickly.

'Please see my guest to the bath-house Imar. Make sure he is thoroughly cleaned.' The servant bowed to Aron and indicated for him to follow.

'Imar.' The servant stopped and turned.

'Yes Princess?'

'There are no women in the men's bath house today are there?'

'I will see to it Princess.'

Aron watched her satisfied grin as she reached for a handful of dried fruit and a cup of water. He turned to follow Imar from the garden and wondered, not for the first time, if he was making the right choice.

****

Sheba took a long, deep breath as Aron greeted her back at the garden.

'Better?' he asked, with a raised eyebrow and a smile that he barely kept in check.

'Much! Shall we go?'

'I am at your service Princess.' Aron offered her his arm.

'If only.' Sheba put her arm in his and pulled him closer.

Aron rolled his eyes and the two laughed.

'Where are we meeting the King?'

'In his private chambers.'

'And you are sure his mother or her servants cannot listen-in there? Is there somewhere more secure?'

'Really! Is this so serious?'

'Yes Sheba. This is not a game. I have already explained, his life and yours depend on it. I'll explain more once we meet with him.'

'There are listening places in his room, but I know where they are. I will make sure they are clear.'

Aron raised an eyebrow. 'Really. You know all the hiding places in the Palace?'

Sheba laughed. 'Every single one of them.

Aron followed the Princess as they wandered through corridors he had never seen before. As Sheba's bodyguard, he had seen most of the women's quarters and the main courtyard, assembly areas and soldiers' barracks, but these places were new to him.

They moved through an open atrium, with corridors leading in various directions. There were hanging plants well above their heads and a fountain, cascading in the centre of the cobble-stoned oasis.

Two guards stood at the entrance of one corridor and the princess guided her bodyguard past them without a sideways glance. The passageway was wide and long, with lanterns every few steps.

The stone walls were ornately engraved with Psalms of King David and where there was no writing, heavy rugs hung, depicting battles won by the Kings of Judah.

They reached a carved, dark wooden door at the end which was as wide as Aron was tall.

'Impressive.' Aron marvelled as Sheba opened the door. It swung with ease, surprising the soldier as he tried to aid the Princess. He gazed at the hinges as they passed through. Trying to keep his mouth closed was more difficult than he expected.

There were no guards stationed outside the King's chambers and only the King occupied the interior. Aron wondered how that was possible. Surely the Captain of the guard would insist on being present.

Sheba closed the door behind them, locking it for good measure. Ahaziah smiled as he watched Aron gaze around the room with a trained eye. He could see by the puzzled look what the soldier was seeing.

'There are very few places I can insist on being free of guards Aron. This is one of them. Here, let me show you.' The King stood from the table and walked around to greet the soldier.

He clasped his forearm in the warriors' grip and smiled earnestly.

'The doors bolt from the inside.' The Princess pointed to the bolt she had just closed, like she was displaying fine china for auction. Both men smiled at her pantomime.

'So if I am not expecting guests, I keep them secure. There are a number of secret passages that access these rooms and I have a bell, which I can ring should the need arise. If rung, the guards that you saw when entering my private wing will come to my aid via the tunnels.'

'Very impressive your Grace. But what if someone you know, whom you have invited into your quarters were to do the unthinkable?'

The King rubbed his chin thoughtfully. 'I allow very few in here unattended Aron. I guess if I make a mistake in my judgement of character, then I would pay the price.'

Aron smiled at Ahaziah's honesty.

'Please, let us sit in a more comfortable setting. The King led the Princess and Aron to the back of the long private meeting room. They passed under a wide stone archway and Aron marvelled at even more decorative artworks.

As they passed through, they entered a luxurious parlour, full of carved stone benches and soft cushions spread out around the floor. Up on the dais was a huge bed, large enough to sleep ten kings. Draped around it were sheer curtains and more walls adorned with woven linen and hanging rugs.

The King waved them to the lounges with an open hand. A low table covered in cold roasted meat, vegetables, crushed chickpeas and wine sat in the centre of one group of lounges.

'You entertain often?' Aron tried to keep his mouth closed as he took in the opulence of the room. The ceiling was so high, he could barely make out the designs on the gold tiles that lined it.

'Not very often anymore. I moved into these chambers after our father died.' The King shrugged with what appeared to be embarrassment. 'I lost myself in here for a few years, making the most of what was left of my youth. But once I realised I needed to take over from my mother and rule Judah, my days of entertainment ceased.'

'Did you know of the secret passageways when your brother *entertained* in here?' Aron looked at Sheba with obvious interest.

'Of course.' The Princess smiled innocently.

'Now that explains a lot.'

The King smiled at the exchange. 'Come, what is so urgent that you must speak with me without my mother?'

Aron looked to Sheba and nodded. She understood his request. She did not take a seat, instead, she wandered to the top of the dais, pulled on a panel behind the large bed and opened a passage way. She disappeared from their sight.

Aron waited patiently, while the King frowned at the unusual level of security. 'What is going on?'

'I will explain in a moment your Grace.

A sound made Aron jump to his feet. A curtain near the arched stone entrance fluttered and Aron made to move toward it until Sheba emerged.

She smiled at his unease. 'You could have warned me.' He grumbled without really being annoyed.

'And where would the fun be in that?' She giggled. 'There is no-one listening.'

'Good.' Aron returned to his seat. Sheba made her way to the lounge, collecting two clay mugs of wine before taking her place alongside her bodyguard. She handed one to Aron and took a deep drink from the other.

'Shall we begin?' the King instructed.

'I am here not only to request you join Jehoram in Jezeel but to honour a promise I made to your Grandmother.' Aron waited a moment before continuing, taking the opportunity to drink some wine himself. He suddenly felt ill at ease with his plan.

'Go on.' The King's impatience was growing. 'What did Jezebel have to say?'

'She believes the Goddess Asherah has shared a vision with her.'

'That is blasphemy Aron. Her wayward worship of Baal and his consort have caused enough trouble for our family.' Ahaziah kept his voice calm. In reality, he had no concern about Jezebel's behaviour, but keeping up the pretence was an important political strategy.

'I am not here to banter over your Grandmother's virtues your Grace. The vision she shared is of this Kingdom being under threat. The reason I do not share this with your mother at present is because much to your Grandmother's concern, your mother may be at the centre of the threat.'

'That is absurd. My Mother would do anything to keep the peace in this Kingdom.' Ahaziah's tone was defensive, but he remained calm.

'Not if you are not present your Grace.'

Sheba had been stunned into silence at the mere mention of the Goddess, but she found her voice quickly. 'Your mother has been unwell Ahaziah. She has been to the temple of Baal often of late and when she returns, as is the case tonight she is not exactly in her right mind.'

'And you think Grandmother talking of visions from Asherah is any less concerning?'

'Why not let Aron explain, then we can discuss this calmly.'

Ahaziah took a breath and nodded his consent.

'As visions can be, Jezebel did not have all the pieces but what she did know is that Sheba must seek refuge with the temple Priest Jehoiada.'

'Refuge from what?' The King sat forward on his seat to refill his cup of wine.

'Fire, death. Jezebel was not sure but it happens while you visit with your uncle.'

'Then I will not leave.' Ahaziah poured himself a cup of wine and almost drained it in one mouthful.

'But your Grace. You must.'

Sheba placed a warning hand on Aron's arm and he realised he had just given the king an order.

'I apologise if my manner offends. I am a mere soldier, not a politician or dignitary, but I must be blunt. Your Uncle is not recovering as well as we had hoped. He is convalescing, not resting in Jezeel but the Zealots are plotting something. He will need your aid. I have seen his General, Jehu in Judah already, meeting with the High Priest.'

'That ends the discussion then. What you have said is even more reason for me to stay here. If I leave, I risk losing Judah and how is Sheba to refuge with the Priest if he is involved?

'Leave Jehoiada to me you Grace. If you do not go, you risk losing Israel to Jehu.'

'There are no winners in what you are proposing Aron. If I leave, I risk losing Judah, if I stay, we risk losing Israel.'

'I am sorry your Grace.' Aron put down his cup and as delicious as the food looked, he could not bring himself to eat any of it.

'Why would the Goddess of the Canaanites help us, the people of Yahweh? Surely it is a trick?' The King rubbed his chin. His finely manicured beard was trimmed low over his face and he rolled the end of it in his fingers until it formed a thin point.

'Asherah has not helped us yet.' Sheba interrupted the King's thought. 'I have no intentions of taking refuge with the Priest and why on earth would I need to hide from Thaliah?'

'Jezebel said you would know why when the time came. As for taking refuge with the Priest, well that is what a wife does, she goes to be with her husband when she is in danger.' Aron waited for his words to filter into the Princess's mind.

'What husband?'

The King sat back on his lounge and took a sip of his wine. He knew this was a serious matter but watching Aron squirm was entertaining.

'I thought you were calling me here to ask for my sister's hand. I was planning on politely declining of course—a man of your station and all, but this is priceless.'

'What are you talking about Ahaziah?' Sheba was getting angry and more confused by the moment.

'Jezebel's vision was clear about one thing. You are to marry the High Priest.' Aron dropped his head to hide his face but even more so, not to see Sheba's.

'How dare you! You asked me to arrange this meeting. You ambushed me.' The Princess stood to leave. 'I will never forgive you Aron.'

Aron was expecting it, but never-the-less the pain in his heart stung more than the slap. He did not try to explain himself. The Princess waited for an argument that never came. She finally turned and left the room, slamming the large wooden door not once, but twice before leaving.

 **Chapter 9**

'That could have gone better.' The King watched Aron's face. They were of a similar age, Aron possibly a few years older. Ahaziah felt for the man. 'She will calm down.'

Aron tried to speak but the words caught in his throat. The King waited patiently.

'Can you make the arrangements for her marriage?'

'If that is what you want.'

'It is not what I want but your Grandmother was very clear. Her life depends on it.'

'Why?'

'Because if Jezebel's vision comes to fruition, your mother will see her relationship with the Priest as leverage and will spare her.'

The King fought his need to defend his mother, recalling his earlier discussion with Sheba. 'She said mother looked to be lining her up to marry the Priest. Maybe Jezebel is right. I pray she is not but there is no denying she has had a special relationship with Asherah for many years.'

'What do you mean?' Aron looked up from his hands and finally rubbed his face where the Princess had hit him.

'I am a follower of Yahweh, do not misunderstand me Aron but the gods of the common people are real. Elijah proved that Baal was not as powerful as Yahweh, but that does not mean he does not exist.'

'I think of the battle of the gods like the battle of Kings your Grace. Way above my station.' Aron smiled as the King began to chuckle.

****

Sheba sat on the ground in the garden, her long, dark hair spread out like a fan behind her. The light of day was fading quickly behind the tall stone walls as the Princess viciously tore the grass from the ground by the handful.

'You cannot throw a tantrum child. You are too old for that now.'

Sheba looked up toward the woman's voice. Her face was hidden in the silhouette of the dying sun. 'Who are you to give *me* orders?'

Sheba knew she sounded over-indulged, but she could not stop herself, her anger was so great.

The woman sat down next to her and Sheba gasped. The figure before her was beautiful beyond words. Her long hair was the colour of gold and her eyes as clear as water. There was a glow around her and the Princess felt as though her skin were tingling.

'Some call me an angel, others a Goddess. Both are correct in a way. My name is Asherah.'

Sheba pulled on the final tuft of grass and held it in her hand, suddenly unsure of what to do with it.

'You have caused my family a great deal of pain Goddess. Why should I listen to you?'

Asherah reached out and touched the Princess's clenched fist. 'Do I look as though I intended to cause pain?'

'It is not about what you look like Asherah. It is about why my father died. He died protecting you.'

'Your father was a great man Sheba. He wanted to see peace amongst his people, not war. It is unfortunate that humanity cannot abide peace it seems.'

'Of course we can. It is the gods that fight for supremacy. We are just caught in the cross-fire.'

'We fight at times, but Yahweh does not. He is beyond that kind of ego. Some of my brethren in the eternal realm fear our Father might love humanity more than us, so they seek to cause you harm. While some of your brethren believe they must fight for the gods, so they do harm to those that do not follow their ways. We do not need you to fight for us Sheba.'

'Why are you telling me this? Why are you even here?' Sheba threw the handful of grass aside and stood to leave.

'Because your Grandmother asked me to come.'

The Princess froze on the spot, looking down at the still seated Goddess. 'Her vision. I know. I will not marry the Priest. I will not!'

'You are a Princess. You have always known your marriage would not be of your choosing.'

'I am, I was before, so far down the royal line I thought no-one would care what I did.'

'The Queen-Mother likely does not care about you, but she certainly would want to secure a politically favourable alliance.'

'But it is not she who wants to marry me to the Priest. It is, it is Aron. I just cannot understand it. I thought…It does not matter what I thought does it?' She shook her head, trying to hold back her tears.

Asherah stood and wrapped the girl in her arms. 'It always matters, but you have a special destiny and Jehoiada is a part of that.'

'What destiny?' Sheba pushed away, to look the Goddess in the eye.

'You will know when the time comes.'

'That is what Grandmother said. Why do you not just tell me?' She sighed loudly and the Goddess smiled knowingly.

'Because I cannot meddle in the choices you make Sheba and make no mistake, this will still be your choice. If you run away and do not marry the Priest—if you choose not to act when the time comes to fulfil your destiny—then it will be your choice, as Yahweh decrees.'

'I thought you and Yahweh were enemies?'

'No. We are far from enemies my child.'

'Then why do the Zealots hate my family for allowing Grandmother to follow you?'

'Because they are human.'

# Chapter 10

Sheba ignored the knock at her door. It was too early in the morning and she had not enjoyed her rest. Instead, she had awoken wrapped in her sheets like an Egyptian mummified corpse.

The knock came again. 'Go away, whoever you are!'

The door knob rattled and the Princess suddenly looked around for her robe. 'Do not *dare* come in here!'

Servants rarely entered her quarters unless called for and Sheba could think of no-one with the gall to come in uninvited.

'Just let me in Sheba.' Aron knocked again, this time more determinedly. 'I know you are angry, but we do not have time for your childish games.'

'Childish! Who on earth do you think you are?' Sheba reached the door in a few large, purposeful steps and tore it open as though it were feathers from a turkey. She was face to face with Aron, staring him down with a snarly expression before she realised what she had done.

He stood before her, leaning on the frame with one hand on his hip and a broad smile on his face.

'You! Ahhh! You are so infuriating Aron.'

'I knew you would open the door once you let your temper get the better of you. Can I come in?'

'No! I am not even half decent. If you must disturb my sleep, the least you can do is give a girl time to make herself respectable.'

'You look fine to me. We have training to do. You are only going to end up hot and sweaty in any case. Come on.' Her bodyguard pulled her gently by the wrist. 'Follow me.'

'No! Seriously! I still have my sleeping wear on under this robe and I cannot possibly train in a robe. Wait outside. I will change.'

Aron stepped back outside and sat on the stone bench that lined the wall of the Princess's rooms.

Sheba fussed with her hair and finally decided a braid was the only sensible option. She hastily pulled her long dark locks into place and tied them with a leather band. She then changed into a light tunic and quickly tied on her sandals.

She opened the door and Aron jumped to attention. Then laughed at his own reaction. 'Just like old times Sheba.'

'Hardly.' The Princess began to walk purposefully toward the soldiers' barracks for training.

Aron reached out and grabbed her firmly by the wrist. 'Wait Sheba. We need to talk.' He looked down at her hand, avoiding the intense gaze he knew was spitting fire at him right now.

'No, we need to train. The barracks or the King's courtyard?'

Aron looked up at her steely gaze and decided now was not the time. 'The King's courtyard. You are too old to be training in front of all the soldiers now.'

'What does that mean?' Sheba took a big breath and pursed her lips as thought holding back a tirade of insults.

'You really have been sheltered. It means I do not have the energy to fight you and the entire legion of soldiers who will be far too distracted by you.'

Sheba relaxed and smiled, nodded her understanding and took the lead to the King's courtyard.

****

'How dare you make a decision like this without consulting me?' Thaliah's eyes were bloodshot and her appearance a little unkempt. Ahaziah wondered about his sister's words and concern furrowed his brow.

His mother misunderstood the look for weakness and continued her tirade. 'You are far too young to be deciding who Sheba marries. You are not even married yourself yet.'

'Mother! The decision is made. You are not the Queen any longer. Your reign here is done. I appreciate your service to Judah but we are moving in troubled times now. The last thing we need is for you to interfere with my decision making.'

'I am fully aware of the times we move in and I am still your Regent.'

'I no longer need a Regent. I am old enough to rule. Besides, you had planned to marry Sheba to the Priest in any case. It was obvious to her, she said as much when I told her of the betrothal.'

'I had said nothing of the sort.' Thaliah's brow creased, deep in thought of who might have betrayed her.

'You apparently did not need to. What deal did you make with Jehoiada? I need to know exactly what he is expecting.'

Thaliah suddenly felt uncomfortable. She had thought her movements had gone unnoticed. *Did Ahaziah know about her meetings with the Baal Priest too?*

'I promised her to him. That is all he wanted.'

'In return for what? What was he to give you?'

'Nothing. I simply asked him to remember he would never have gained a Princess's hand without me.'

****

Jehoiada knelt at the foot of the altar. He kissed his thumb and forefinger and let the prayer leave his lips. He could not recall how or why, but somehow he had managed to make himself an ally to both the Queen-Mother, a known worshipper of Baal and her very public enemy, the Zealots of Yahweh.

When Jehu came to him, he had thought the man was there on King's business at first, but as the situation unfolded, he realised it was much more treacherous than that. He was now not only conspiring with a Baal worshipper, but was possibly involved in treason.

The sweat dripped from his brow eventhough the morning was cool and the High Priest felt close to fainting.

The sound of someone clearing their throat made Jehoiada almost jump from his skin.

He spun around to see one of his altar boys waiting to gain his attention.

'What is it Ezra?' He did not attempt to hide his frustration.

'The King has sent word. He wishes you to attend his chambers. Immediately.'

The Priest stood open-mouthed a moment, but quickly recovered. 'Very well. Get along with you now. You have chores to do.' Jehoiada watched the boy retreat before allowing himself to breath. His stomach felt like it was turning inside out and his mouth was suddenly extraordinarily dry. What did Ahaziah know? Should he warn him?

 **Chapter 11**

Jehoiada followed the guard as he made his way through the outer gardens of the palace to meet with the King. He had expected to be greeted in the main atrium or possibly the great hall, but as he looked around, he realised none of the surroundings were familiar.

The pathway meandered through rows of flowers, green grass the likes of which the Priest had never seen, not even in the main palace entrance and there were so many tall trees laden with dates and many exotic fruits.

The sound of clashing weapons reached his ears and the beads of sweat that had been running down his back, now spread to his palms. He took a deep breath, trying to calm himself.

As he rounded the corner of the stone walkway, past a small grove of palm trees that lined a deep dark pond, he saw the cause of the commotion. Sheba swung her weapon gently in a circle around her wrist, while her opponent watched on carefully, crouched ready to attack.

At first the Priest thought the Princess was in mortal danger, but he quickly realised the man opposite her was the same soldier he had recently introduced to the King, the same man who challenged him about Jehu.

He was not sure which was more distracting, the thought that the King knew about Jehu or Sheba. She wore a short tunic of light, almost see through fabric, tied at the waist with a wide leather belt. Her dark hair was tied back in a long braid and her bronze legs shone in the early morning sun.

The Priest quickly averted his eyes when the soldier nodded in his direction. He blushed and fixed his eyes on the intricate stone work before him. The sound of steel on steel sent shudders down his spine. *Who on earth trained the Princess to fight? Why?* He wondered silently.

****

'You should say hello you know.' Aron nodded in the Priest's direction as he passed.

'Do not give me reason to use this weapon in earnest.' Sheba frowned at her opponent, who only grinned in reply.

'You really believe you can?'

The Princess did not wait for Aron to finish. She feigned a jab to her right, before sending a back swing toward the soldier's left shoulder.

'Whoa up there Princess. You do not want to take me out of action on our very first day back at training.'

'I thought you said I would not be able to.'

'I have been known to be wrong, occasionally.'

Aron moved as he spoke, knowing the compliment would put Sheba off guard. His sword struck flat on her left buttock, causing her to grimace, but she did not falter. Instead, she moved in closer to Aron and shoulder-charged his undefended side.

He was thrown off balance but she was not heavy enough to take him from his feet. He recovered quickly, blocking her elbow with his left forearm as she tried to bring it up into his chin.

'You have been practising.' Aron stated without any hint of mockery. 'I am impressed. Who with?'

'Why? Are you jealous?' The Princess stepped back a few paces, giving herself some breathing room.

'Possibly.' Aron watched the Princess carefully.

'I practise with no-one.'

'Well that is good news.' Aron smiled but the Princess was focussed. She moved to her right, looking for an opening, but Aron tossed his sword to his other hand, blocking her lunge easily. With the twist of his wrist, he wrapped his blade around hers and it flew to her far right, entirely out of reach.

'What now?' Sheba challenged. 'You have broken my heart. Why not kill me?' She dropped her head and allowed her shoulders to slump forward, defeated in body and soul.

Aron was taken aback. He lowered his weapon and moved to comfort the Princess, but as he made to wrap his arm around her shoulder, she lifted her head quickly, knocking him hard in the chin. His teeth cracked together as he fell back, losing balance, his sword slipping from his grip. The Princess used his momentum to bring him down on his back, quickly pinning his hands under her knees as she straddled him.

'I am so very glad we did not do this in the soldiers' training ground.' Aron grinned.

'Why? Too embarrassing?' Sheba challenged him, her knees pushing firmly, her thighs tight around his hips.

'No. More along the lines of too unseemly.'

'What are…' The Princess had no time to finish her question. Aron flipped her effortlessly onto her back, reversing the positions. He held her hands next to her head with his and loomed over her, still smiling.

She struggled under his weight, trying to bite his arm, but she could not reach him.

'Get off me!' She growled like a trapped desert cat.

'Why? No-one can see us.'

'Just get off me, please.' She stopped struggling and tears appeared in the corners of her eyes.

'Are those real tears or another ruse?' Aron watched carefully, trying to judge just how far to push the Princess.

Sheba turned her head away and Aron knew then it was not an act. 'You fought well. Do not be hard on yourself. I am more skilled than I was when I trained you. I have fought many battles Sheba. Really!' He rolled from the Princess, jumped to his feet and offered her his hand.

She shook her head, instead sitting up she pulled her knees to her chest and hid her face behind them crossing her arms protectively.

'Sheba, talk to me.' Aron knelt down next to her on one knee. 'Come, it is time to break our fast in any case. We can talk in your rooms while we eat.'

The Princess shook with tears of rage. Aron could not tell the difference. Instead of

waiting for her to rise, he picked her up. She
was a head smaller than him and likely close to
half his weight.

'Put me down.' She managed to speak,
but her words were barely a whisper and she
did not struggle.

'Shush now. I might have been too tough
on you for the first day back.' He spoke into her
hair quietly as he carried her to her rooms. 'I
just want to make sure you are ready.'

****

'High Priest. Welcome. You look like
you have seen a ghost.' The King stood from
his long table and walked around to welcome
the man into his private chambers.

Jehoiada looked around the foreign room.
It was large, with an extremely long wooden
table, surrounded by tall backed chairs, covered
in soft woven linen. The King offered him a
seat, even going so far as to pull it away from
the table for him.

He then took a seat opposite, offering
him a cup of water and indicating to help
himself to the platter of food before him.

The King's manner should have settled
him, but instead he was growing more nervous
by the moment. He forced himself to speak.
'Your summons was unexpected your Grace
and I have never seen this part of the palace. I

am simply a little unfamiliar with my surroundings.' His voice was surprisingly clear and steady.

'I have been talking with my mother.' The King watched him closely and he tried not to give anything away with his expression. 'It seems she has been alluding to promises she is not in any position to keep. I apologise. She was Regent for some time before I came to the throne. Old habits, you know.' Ahaziah shrugged apologetically.

The Priest nodded, suddenly feeling that bad news was only moments away.

'In any case. It appears she has chosen you to wed my sister.' The King waited. Jehoiada realised he must have been gauging his reaction, but he was unable to hide his excitement. 'Now ordinarily Sheba being so far down the royal line would have been given a little more choice in her suiter, so I am afraid that she might not be very receptive to you at first, but please, give her a little time, should you wish to accept her hand of course.'

Ahaziah smiled politely, but as he watched the Priest's eyes distinctly light up, he knew the answer.

'Of course your Grace. It is a great honour you bestow upon me.'

'Now not so quickly. You seem to have grown close to my mother, but *she* is not making this offer. Do you understand?'

Jehoiada nodded, but his brow furrowed as he wondered what was to come next. Did Ahaziah know of the usurper? Did he know of his own involvement?

'Relax Jehoiada. There are only two conditions I will add, well three to be more precise. Sheba is to be your absolute first priority, right behind Yahweh of course.' The Priest chuckled nervously, but nodded, his mind still racing with excitement and unanswered questions.

'That goes without saying your Grace. I will honour her. You have my vow as a man of the temple.'

Ahaziah nodded and smiled. The Priest relaxed.

'You are to protect my son. He is the only heir of both Judah and Israel. You understand? No matter your personal feelings; no matter who comes against you, you will protect Joash.'

Jehoiada frowned once more. He had to give his word, but how could he with his knowledge? He knew Jehu wanted to school the boy, but still, conflict could bring any outcome.

Ahaziah noticed the hesitation. 'Is this a problem?'

'Of course not, your Grace. It is just a great responsibility. I was not expecting it.' The King nodded once more.

'Thirdly. You are not, under any circumstances to do my mother's bidding. This is not negotiable. Do you understand and agree to all three conditions?'

Jehoiada took a deep breath, realising he had barely taken a breath throughout the King's list of demands. The Queen-Mother frightened him to some extent and he knew that to go against her, much like Jehu, could prove fatal but the prize for his courage was Sheba.

He nodded his consent before he could change his mind. 'Of course. All three of your commands will be honoured your Grace. I am truly blessed with such a responsibility. When can I meet with Sheba?' He fidgeted like one of his altar boys and forced himself to stop.

'As is customary, we will arrange a wedding feast. I was supposed to visit my uncle, but he will have to wait another few weeks before I can make that trip.'

The Priest suddenly realised what Jehu would have to say about his involvement in delaying the General's plans. The colour drained form his face and the King stopped speaking suddenly.

'It is fine Jehoiada, you can still meet with my sister before the wedding feast, but her bodyguard will be present at all times.'

Jehoiada recovered quickly realising the King mistook his sudden shock with not being able to see Sheba.

'Is there a reason why I saw her fighting with her bodyguard, I assume it was him, as I came in? Most unseemly for a young woman.'

'You will find Sheba is not an ordinary young woman and I suggest you do not try to stop her or control her. It would definitely not be in keeping with our first condition of your marriage.'

The Priest frowned and the King smiled knowingly. He rose from the chair and slapped the man on the shoulders. 'It is fine Jehoiada. She is a Princess. Just give her everything she wants and life will be perfect.'

Chapter 12

Aron left Sheba to find a servant. He noticed a young man, no more than twelve cutting flowers in the garden.

'Can you ask the cook to prepare the Princess some food? I will take some too.'

The boy creased his brow with an obvious lack of recognition but quickly decided he was in no position to argue. He nodded and bowed to leave.

'Have someone deliver the food to her rooms.' The boy turned, a knowing smile crept across his face. Aron chose not to clarify his position. The boy was only a servant, what harm could he do jumping to the wrong conclusion?

He turned and made his way quickly back to the Princess. She was wrapped up in her bedspread, still crying to herself.

Aron sat at the end of the bed, lost for words. He patted her leg from on top of the fabric, but she pulled it back.

'Sheba. If you do not tell what is wrong, I am not able to fix it.'

The silence grew and Aron paced, wondering what she could possibly be so distraught about. Her training was going well. She remembered basically everything he had ever taught her, maybe even some he had not. She was confident, aggressive when she needed to be and quite strong for a small woman.

A knock on the door brought Aron out of his contemplation. He looked at Sheba, still wrapped protectively under her bedding, before opening the door.

A full busted woman in her middle years walked in, trying to keep her eyes cast down. She laid a full platter of food on the bed chest and retreated, but not before noticing the Princess wrapped in her bedding. She tried unsuccessfully to keep the surprise from her eyes and Aron almost tried to explain she was ill, but instead decided to let the matter sort itself out.

He closed the door behind the servant and locked the bolt in place. He sat alongside the food tray and began preparing something to eat. He took a large piece of flat bread, layered it with thick goat cheese and placed small pieces of dried figs and dates on top. He scattered some greens on top and wrapped it into a roll.

'Here, you should eat something. You have likely just exhausted yourself.' He sat on the side of the bed and nudged Sheba. She was not asleep. She was ignoring him and his patience was growing thin.

'What would your father say right now? Stop this Sheba. You are being stubborn. Eat something.'

Sheba sat up so quickly that Aron nearly dropped her food on the floor. She grabbed it out of his hand and began eating it like a starved animal.

'You…you have no idea….' She tried to speak through mouthfuls of food and Aron smiled triumphantly. 'Wipe that stupid grin... off... your face.'

He made to speak and Sheba put her finger up in front of his face. 'You…,' she finished her mouthful. 'When you came back, I thought you came for me. Now you are marrying me off to an old man and on top of that, you are my bodyguard and that means I am forced to spend nearly every waking hour looking at you, touching you, smelling you. Are you a sadist? Seriously! What were you expecting?'

Aron watched the Princess and sighed. 'It is not easy for me either Sheba. When I left, we were still young. I cared deeply for you, but you are a Princess and I am a soldier.' Sheba opened her mouth to speak and Aron placed his finger gently on her lips. 'Let me finish, please.' She nodded, but kissed his finger seductively.

'Please! Do not make this any harder than it already is. I told you before, I will not spoil you for a proper marriage.'

'Why not? You said yourself the Priest wants to marry me, likely for prestige more than anything else.'

'I did not say that. You cannot risk him embarrassing you in public. You might end up banished, or worse, stoned to death.'

'Ahaziah would never allow it.'

'Sheba, if what your Grandmother saw comes to be, you may not have your brother's protection. I am doing this for you. You must see that!'

'I do not care.' Sheba threw the bedspread aside and knelt next to Aron, slowly untying her leather belt as she kissed him.

He returned the kiss with a passion he had buried, but as his ears roared with his rising blood, he moved away, and stood up, removing himself from the Princess's grip as she pulled her tunic free.

'Sheba, I beg you.' He turned on his heel and headed for the door. 'Please forgive me,' he blurted out before pulling the door closed behind him. He leant against it, his face flushed and his mind racing with images of the Princess's naked body replaying over and over.

****

Jehoiada had returned to the temple for barely enough time to catch his breath before the Queen-Mother tracked him down.

'Jehoiada, I see all your dreams are coming true.'

'The King has been very gracious to me.'

'The King!' Thaliah scoffed. 'Your marriage is my doing and I suggest you recall that when the time comes.'

Jehoiada's mind raced. All he ever wanted to do was be a priest, yet suddenly, he was finding himself embroiled in politics. He was unsure if he was loathing or loving it, but something in the Queen-Mother's tone warned him to play along, eventhough he had made a vow to Ahaziah.

'Of course Thaliah.' Jehoiada bowed reverently. 'I have no intentions of forgetting about your involvement.'

The Queen-Mother watched the Priest intently, trying to decide just how loyal the man would be, but concluded now was not the time to push him. That time was when she ruled in Judah and her son had taken the throne of Israel.

She nodded her head, finally deciding to accept him at his word. Thaliah felt a cool breeze filter through the temple. It was not unpleasant and the smell it cast was familiar.

She planted a smile on her lips and looked at Jehoiada. 'I will see you at the wedding then Priest.' She lifted her long robe in her hand as she swung around to leave. Thaliah frowned as the breeze seemed to push her from the temple as it fluttered at her back.

****

'That woman can be repulsive.' Asherah spoke aloud.

'I do not know sister. I have grown to like her.' Asherah swung around to find Moloch smiling at her back.

'I was not talking to you. I was making a personal observation.'

'If your logic holds Asherah, you cannot blame Thaliah, she is innocent of my manipulation of her.'

'Oh shut up. Some humans are not entitled to that argument being held in their defence. That woman is one of them.'

'You are changing sister. You are the one who always tells me the humans are not inherently evil, that the fallen are at fault. Yet, Thaliah has never met any of the fallen.'

'No, but you are getting very close brother. It is only a matter of time before you blur the line too widely and father decides he should have thrown you into the earthly realm with the fallen.'

'What makes you think we are not both fallen Asherah? We meddle in the lives of the humans every day.'

'Just go away Moloch. You and I have very different ideas of meddling. You do not show yourself. You hide behind the façade of humans and play pretend. When I reveal myself, I say who I am. I do not lie or deceive. These are the methods used by the Lord of the Fallen, not of Father.'

'So old and yet still so naïve. I wish I knew how Michael and the other Archangels managed to keep you so misguided.'

'I am not misguided. I thought after you helped us against Dagon that you had finally seen the error of your ways, but I was mistaken. You are still scheming to stop the Redeemer.' Asherah opened her arms wide, allowing her wings to unfold. She leapt into the air and rolled as she flew high away from Moloch's words.

He was always so talented at infuriating her. She wanted to hate him, but was unable to force such strong emotions. The sun disappeared behind a cloud and the Goddess chased it, flying through the soft, moist fluffy fog as she pushed on into the Eternal Realm above.

She needed to refuge away from the world below. The people were oblivious to the war that continued to rage around them. They had been told the stories of the fallen angels and believed that was the entire story, but they did not know the war continued, hidden amongst the angels that still lived in manufactured peace.

Asherah flew through the veil that held back the magical realm the angel's called home. She thought about where to go and replenish her energy. Her garden in Jericho had been destroyed when the walls fell. She could return to her father's house, with her sisters Astarte and Anath, but that would only highlight the continued tension she was trying to avoid.

Instead, she flew toward a waterfall that fell from the Heavens, through the veil into the mountains below.

She felt isolated, as though she were the only one who saw existence the way she did. Their Father remained distant, communicating through his Archangels, but never allowing Asherah or her brethren to hear Him. All she had to guide her was her own thought and she had to believe she was created by the Father for His purpose, so her thoughts and therefore her actions were His.

'They need more Father. We need more! More than guessing your plans. More than instructions from Michael or Gabriel. More than prophecies from anointed Prophets that claim to be the only way we can truly know your mind.'

'That is why the bringer of peace, the Redeemer must come Asherah.'

Asherah had not uttered a word aloud. She had been flying and gliding through the veil toward the waterfall, mulling over her frustration. She stopped mid-flight and hovered in the air, her hair floating in the weightless space between worlds.

'Who are you?' She whispered to the voice.

The air around her shimmered and Gabriel appeared. He was half as tall as her again and his broad, bare chest bore the markings of his rank.

He smiled at her surprised face. 'You thought I was Father?'

'I hoped.' Asherah looked down, trying to avoid his gaze.

'He hears you Goddess. Why do you think I am here? Why do you think I know your inner thoughts?'

'Why does He not come Himself?' Asherah challenged, suddenly angry but unsure who with, herself or her Father.

'Because you can already hear Him if you choose sister. He is here.' Gabriel touched her chest gently. 'Not here', he moved on to her temple, tapping it with his finger.

'I would like to believe you Gabriel but if that is true, then Moloch hears a different Father to me.'

The Angel laughed aloud, his eyes sparkling with delight. 'Moloch does what he does for selfish reasons. He listens to no-one.'

'Then why does Father let him get away with it? I do not understand.' Asherah scowled like a frustrated child and put her hands on her hips, all while her wings moved gently behind her, somehow belying her internal rage.

'It is not your fight Asherah. You must trust the plan is made,' Gabriel stated, his manner suddenly serious.

'So I should do nothing! Let Moloch play his games and Father will fix it with or without me?' Gabriel shrugged. 'See, even you do not know.' Asherah protested.

'There is only the prophecy Asherah. If you chose to aid Father, then do so with love, not with frustration, vengeance or pride.'

Asherah looked deeply into Gabriel's crystal blue eyes and smiled suddenly. 'I see.'

'Do you?' Gabriel challenged, smiling good-naturedly. 'His people, these people,' Gabriel waved his arm to the unseen world below, 'they believe they hear Father and sometimes they do. There are prophetic writings, such as the prophecy of the Redeemer, but sometimes they hear with their own minds. Make sure you are hearing Father's will and not your own sister.'

Asherah smiled as Gabriel placed his hand on her shoulder, squeezing it affectionately. 'I do see. Thank you.'

Gabriel disappeared as quickly as he had arrived. Only a shimmer of light remained where he had been.

Asherah extended her silver wings once more and began to fly again, this time, with a heart much lighter than before.

Chapter 13

Jehu looked up from his desk, an unfinished parchment still lay before him. The soldier stopped at the entrance to the commander's tent, bowed and moved forward with a nod from his General.

'What is it?' The soldier handed the General a rolled parchment which he quickly unwound. He placed it on his desk, with a heavy stone to hold it open while he read.

'I will cut off his hands for this.' The soldier said nothing. He simply stood to attention, his eyes fixed front as he awaited his orders.

Jehu scribbled a note quickly, rolled it and tied it with a piece of leather. He handed it across his desk to the soldier.

'Take this to the High Priest in Judah. Make sure you personally deliver it. Send Isaac in on your way out.'

The soldier nodded, placed the note inside his tunic and saluted before turning to leave. Jehu watched the man leave and let out a heartfelt sigh. He reached for the decanter of wine on his desk and poured a full cup for himself and another for Isaac.

He was placing the decanter back on the table as his most trusted officer entered.

'You requested my presence.'

'I did. We have a delay, one I am not happy about.'

'No delay is a good one General. What is the issue?' Isaac took the offered wine from the General's hand and sat in the only place he could, the lounge beside the General's desk.

Jehu stood and joined him, bringing his cup of wine with him, which he placed on the table that stood before the lounge.

'Jehoiada has gone and gotten himself betrothed, to the Princess no less. Now we must wait on the wedding ceremony before Ahaziah will leave to meet with Jehoram.'

'That is inconvenient.' Isaac's eyebrow rose as his lip twitched.

'Yahweh is angry over that harlot Queen worshipping Baal. We lose every battle because of her heresy. Now our plans are delayed.'

'Maybe Yahweh is not with us after all.' Isaac smiled, knowing the response he was expecting.

'Do not toy with me Isaac. I think you know why I called you here.'

'Of course, you want someone dead, other than Jehoram and Ahaziah of course.' Isaac took a deep gulp of the wine, knowing he would be sent on his way at any moment and he really wanted to drink the wine before he had to go. Jehu's wine was always top shelf.

'Yes, but I still have not decided if it should be the Priest or the Princess.' He took a sip of his wine as this thought manifested. 'Collect some additional men, take them to Judah, ready for our next move. I have given a note to one of my men. He will travel with you. His orders are to deliver the note to the Priest. I will consider our options and send word of who is to die.'

'That is not something I expect should go in a note easily read by a messenger.'

'You always surprise me Isaac.' Jehu nodded and pursed his lips in thought. 'True, very true. Let us call the Priest the 'candle stick' and the Princess 'the dove'.'

'Very well. Before or after the wedding?'

'I am yet to decide.'

Isaac chuckled to himself as he finished the last mouthful of the full-bodied red wine. 'It shall be as you wish General.'

****

Isaac collected two officers and gave them orders as he made his way to his tent. He packed two small leather bags and swung them over his shoulder. His short sword never left his side while he was awake, and sometimes, not even then. He took two short daggers from his belongings and tucked them into a leather strap that hung over his tunic and across his chest.

A quick mental count of all his necessary supplies brought a wicked grin to the man's lips. He wiped it from his face as he left the tent to meet with the two officers who waited patiently outside.

'No need to look so nervous men. Just a quick ride to Jerusalem, another battle or two and we will be back, ready to take leave and enjoy the beds of beautiful women and gorge ourselves on something other than army rations.'

Both men nervously chuckled and turned to follow the General's assassin. 'Collect your men and follow along to Jerusalem but take a wide berth and make camp in the Valley of Kidron. No need to alarm young Ahaziah now is there?'

The officers looked at each other from behind Isaac's back and frowned. One made to ask a question, but the other shook his head fervently. Both men answered in unison. 'Yes Sir.'

****

'No! Not that one either.' Sheba shook her head at the frustrated seamstress. 'I just want something simple.'

'But you are a royal princess my dear. You are to be wed in front of the King, the visiting dignitaries and the Queen-Mother.'

'It is *my* wedding and *I* will choose the dress.'

The middle-aged woman sighed in resignation and left the room to find more rolls of fabric and dresses for the Princess to choose from.

'You really should not take this out on her you know.' Aron sat trying not to smile at Sheba's obvious irritation.

'What are you even here for?' Sheba called out from behind a wide, silk screen as she threw the most recent reject over the beautifully painted fabric.

Aron watched her silhouette as she tried on the next soon-to-be rejected wedding dress.

'I am still your bodyguard.'

'Yes, and I plan on speaking to Ahaziah about that.'

'He is unlikely to take any notice. He honours nearly every one of your whims Princess, but when we last spoke, he understood the need to keep you protected.'

'I am unsure if I can go through with this Aron.' Sheba's tone changed as she walked out from behind the screen, smoothing the dress into place as she spoke.

Aron stared at her, open-mouthed before quickly averting his eyes. The colour was perfect on her. The gold fabric made her bronze skin look smooth and flawless, and her eyes looked like deep, dark rock pools.

'I wish you had a choice.'

'Asherah said I did.' Sheba's gaze penetrated Aron's heart and it took all his strength not to take her in his arms and kiss her, but he did not.

'You have met Asherah?' He suddenly realised what the Princess had said.

'Just after I slapped you actually.' Sheba smiled with slight embarrassment. 'I am sorry about that by the way. You could have warned me though.'

'You would not have taken me.'

'There is truth in that. I want to leave Aron. Asherah said that I could run away, not follow this destiny. Why do I have to give up everything I love and do this?'

She had moved across the room, and was now standing before Aron, who had yet to stand for fear his legs might give way. She reached out and touched his face gently, caressing it with her fingertips. 'Take me away Aron.'

'Sheba.' He took her hand in his and held it to his lips. 'I begged you not to ask me. I want to, with every fibre in my body and every beat of my heart, but that could spell the end of your family-line and risk your life.'

'I have no care for my family legacy.'

'You have to meet Jehoiada properly. Talk with him, then decide.' Aron tried to change the subject.

'But I want *you* Aron. I want to feel your body against mine.'

Aron reached out, his hand sliding along Sheba's body to her thigh. As he moved to stand a sound stopped him. The seamstress cleared her throat and cast her eyes down, but did not say a word.

'She will take this one.' Aron said as he dropped his hand from her side. Sheba mouthed the words *I love you*, before turning to greet the seamstress with a broad smile.

'Yes. I will take this one. It is beautiful.' The seamstress physically jumped with excitement, what she had just seen, forgotten instantly.

'Thank you Princess. Thank you. I am so happy you have found what you are looking for.'

'Yes, me too.' The Princess tried to keep the regret from her voice.

Chapter 14

Jehoiada had never been so excited in his life. Today he would finally be allowed to spend the afternoon with his future wife and his heart raced at the thought.

He fussed with his robe, having finally decided on something less extravagant than his High Priest formal wear. The homespun goat's wool was light and soft to the touch and the Priest hoped so very much that the Princess would like it.

'A message Sir.'

Jehoiada turned to see his young acolyte waiting patiently at the door to his private room. The door was open wide during the day, as was his custom, in case anyone should need to speak with him.

'Bring it to me boy.' The Priest held out his hand impatiently, assuming it must be a note from the Princess.

The boy waited to be dismissed, but Jehoiada was so intent on reading the note, he failed to notice the boy, who fidgeted nervously.

He scanned the words quickly and beads of sweat broke out on his forehead.

Marry her at your own risk Priest!

The note was unsigned. 'Who left this?' Jehoiada challenged the boy.

'A soldier Sir. An officer of the King.' The boy shuffled his feet and cast his eyes down.

'Which King?'

'Israel I think, but I cannot be sure. He may have been a mercenary. His uniform was dirty. Or maybe he came directly from fighting somewhere?'

'Leave me. I have work to do.'

The boy bowed and shuffled from the room, happy to be free of any more questions.

Jehoiada sat down heavily on the hard bench seat that stood against the wall alongside his writing desk. Many a young acolyte had been scolded in this seat and now Jehoiada felt he was about to receive a dressing down of his own.

It had to be from General Jehu. No-one else would threaten him for marrying Sheba. How could he not have realised the General would see his marriage to the Princess as a move against the Zealots?

But he had to understand. Marrying Sheba would ensure she was coached in the faith of her people, and not influenced by her

Grandmother or Stepmother in the ways of Baal. Why would he be against such ideals?

Jehoiada rose and moved to his desk. He had to get word to the General and quickly. He could control his new bride. He would ensure that Judah continued to follow Yahweh if the General would only trust him.

He scribed a note and called his acolyte. The boy would need to search every tavern and see if he could find the messenger, otherwise, Jehoiada was not sure how he was going to get his message to Jehu before the General acted on his threat.

The Priest poured a cup of red wine and drank it down in one long gulp. He planted his hands firmly on the table, willing himself to take deep, slow breaths until his heart stopped beating in his ears. He still had to meet with Sheba and he needed to make the right first impression on the young woman.

****

'I will be here with you the whole time Sheba.' Aron escorted the Princess out of her room to the royal garden. The sun was high and fierce and Sheba allowed the warmth to soak into her stiff and rigid muscles.

'I would rather be out running or training than meeting Jehoiada.'

'Give the man a chance.' Aron coaxed.

'I will try.'

The Princess moved toward a seat under the veranda, away from the direct sunlight. As she entered the shade, she shivered, as though the cool air was iced water.

The stone ground had been meticulously swept clean of leaves and the seats were piled high with brightly coloured cushions of gold, red and orange. There was a table between two lounges that faced each other. It was laid out with fresh fruit, dried dates, nuts, flat bread and soft cheese. A large pitcher of watered wine with beads of condensation rolling down the side, had left a small puddle in the centre of the table.

Aron stood a few paces behind Sheba's lounge and waited for her to take a seat. A servant stood twenty paces away, ready to do her bidding with the wave of a hand.

A tall, thin man with a long beard entered the courtyard. Sheba had met Jehoiada on many occasions, but all formal and all when he was in service to her brother. She had never exchanged words with him, only nodded her acknowledgement.

A servant guided the Priest to the Princess and bowed. 'Jehoiada, High Priest of Judah your highness.' He bowed again and backed away to the other end of the veranda.

Sheba did not stand, instead offered her hand to the Priest who frowned for a moment before taking it gently and kissing the top of her fingers lightly.

Aron smiled at the Priest's confusion. Sheba was making it very clear she was the highest ranked in the room.

'Your Grace, it is a pleasure to finally meet with you. I am sorry this did not happen before your brother announced our betrothal.'

Sheba indicated with her hand for him to take a seat opposite her.

'Can I get you a glass of wine, something to eat?' Sheba offered and the Priest's eyes sparkled.

'That would be most accommodating Princess.'

'You are my guest. It is only good manners.' Aron did not miss Sheba's coolness. She had not offered to be addressed by her name and she made it obvious this was her duty, not her choice.

For a moment, he felt sorry for the Priest, but then the man spoke and ruined it.

'Am I to call you Princess after we are married?'

Sheba passed a small wicker plate with food and a cup of wine to the Priest. Aron could see her jaw muscles tense up and wondered if he should intervene, but waited too long.

'We are not yet married Priest and first names generally represent some sort of familiarity. I have never truly met you. So, let us start from a formal place of respectability, shall we?'

Aron thought the man, accustomed to being in charge, would balk but he remained calm. 'As you wish Princess. You are quite right.'

There was an uncomfortable silence between the two as they both ate and drank, looking over their cup at each other, sizing up the situation and no doubt trying to think of something productive to say.

'Well, we are here to discover more about each other so let us start with the most common of discussions. What are your views on the Zealots?'

Jehoiada nearly choked on his mouthful of wine, but managed to gulp it down without spitting it out. He coughed, placed his hand over his mouth and coughed a few more times before thumping his chest with his fist and finally drawing a calming breath.

Aron remained at ease, standing behind the Princess. The Priest looked up at him almost pleadingly and Aron only shrugged in response.

'Politics and religion are not conversations for young ladies. Surely you can think of something more interesting? What are your hobbies? Perhaps we can talk of those?'

'Actually, both politics and religion are quite prudent when you think about it. The Zealots killed my father, my brothers and sisters all except Ahaziah. If we are to marry, surely I need to understand your views on such matters?'

Jehoiada took a deep breath and sank into the lounge, trying to think of a suitable response. He was involved with the Zealots. He believed Yahweh and only He should reign over Israel and Judah. How on earth was he to answer such a question?'

'Well, let me help you. You met with Jehu in your own temple recently, a known Zealot sympathiser. What did you talk about?'

'You have been spying on me?' Jehoiada's eyes opened wide as he almost whispered his words.

'Not at all. Aron has already told you he saw you with Jehu and it was of course reported to Ahaziah.'

Jehoiada wiped his sweaty palms on his robe and pursed his lips.

'Let us not worry. I think your silence speaks volumes. My brother said you were surprised to see me training with Aron.' The Princess looked over her should at Aron and winked. 'Wherever I go, Aron here goes.' She returned her gaze to the Priest and indicated her bodyguard with her thumb and the tilt of her head.

'Wherever you go? Surely not after we are married?' Jehoiada was growing more distressed by the moment and Aron could tell Sheba was beginning to enjoy this meeting.

'If there is still any threat against my family, as there is with the Zealot fanatics, then yes, he will accompany me. Surely you understand?'

'I do.' Jehoiada suddenly realised he had to make a choice—the Princess or the Zealots and he was now more confused than ever.

'I will marry you Jehoiada, for the good of my family but only if you remove yourself from any further contact with the Zealot faction. If you cannot do that, then I would rather risk banishment than marry you.'

'You have made yourself very clear Princess.' Jehoiada placed his cup carefully on the table before him and stood to leave. He bowed reverently, 'I hope we can talk again soon Princess. It has been most enlightening.'

'Of course. I look forward to it.' Sheba waved for the servant who had patiently waited on her needs. 'Please show the High Priest the way out.' The servant nodded.

Jehoiada bowed again, to Aron and the Princess and followed the servant out of the courtyard as fast as possible.

Aron waited until the Priest was out of earshot before speaking. 'I thought I might need to school you on how to handle that man, but you do not need me at all. A few little pieces of insight and you used them perfectly.'

He moved around to sit alongside Sheba and she let out an anxious breath.

'That took every bit of my self-control, really it did. He wants me barefoot and pregnant on our wedding night. He did not even deny his involvement with the men who killed my father, my family.'

Aron wanted to wrap his arm around the Princess, but he did not. Instead, he moved closer and spoke in hushed tones. 'You understand how dangerous this is now? Why your Grandmother sent me?'

'I do, and I am forever grateful. I also understand why I must marry the Priest. Keep your friends close and your enemies even closer.'

Chapter 15

'Are we planning a wedding then sister?' Ahaziah tickled the ribs of the little dark headed toddler that sat on his lap. Giggles exploded from his chest as every part of his body wriggled to avoid his father's fingers.

'I still do not like the man, but yes, I will marry him. I understand my duty.'

'I am sorry Sheba. I had really hoped you would like him. You do not have to love him, or even find him attractive, but you do need to tolerate him.'

'As long Aron is with me, I can tolerate just about anything.'

'Be careful Sheba. The servants are talking.'

'About what?'

'About you and your bodyguard. You need to be more discreet.'

'We have done nothing wrong.'

'So, Aron being in your chambers when you were naked in bed is nothing wrong?'

Sheba took a deep breath, ready to explode her full fury when she suddenly realised what must have happened. 'I was not naked. I was crying my eyes out and Aron was trying to convince me I had to marry the Priest. He was a complete gentleman.'

'You seem upset about that.' Ahaziah smiled. 'Joash, get the ball for dada.' He rolled a skin filled with seeds across the grass and the toddler, barely walking, waddled after it.

'I am I guess, but he is right, I cannot be sullied for the wedding.'

'Rubbish. You are a Princess. I heard you put the man in his place. Good on you. I gave him three conditions to marrying you and your happiness was the first. I also warned him as a Princess, you were used to getting your own way and if he wanted to marry you, he had best get used to it.'

'What does that mean?'

'You decide sister, you decide. Our role takes sacrifices, many of them. Take Joash there. He is my pride and joy. He is not even the true heir, one of his many sister's children could easily rule when I am gone, but I do not care. Zabiah was the one I loved Sheba. She died giving birth to him, so he is everything to me.'

'It is different for you Ahaziah. Kings can have as many consorts as they want. You will not get stoned to death.'

'Aron would never let that happen to you.'

'What are you implying?'

'I am implying nothing. Just remember, sometimes we have to do what we have to, in order to survive the pressure our title brings.'

Joash squealed and Ahaziah jumped at the sound. The boy was face down on the stone pathway, leading from the King's private courtyard. He looked at his father's frightened face and his lip began to quiver, followed quickly by a howl as tears started to run down his cheeks.

Sheba jumped up with her brother to aid the distraught toddler, just as his nursemaid came running from the opposite direction.

'We have him Rivkah. He is fine. Just a bump.' Ahaziah spoke as he lifted his son into his strong arms, cradling his head onto his shoulder as the tears wet his tunic.

'I am going to miss him when I go to Jezeel.'

'You are still going? With everything that is rumoured?'

'I have to help Jehoram.'

'When will you leave?'

'The morning after your ceremony. I cannot miss your wedding feast. We have not had a wedding in the palace for too long. You are the last royal of our line Sheba. After you, it is only my children and yours who will be married in this palace.'

'I have to sleep with the Priest to have children.' A shiver ran down her spine. 'I am still not sure I can do that.' She laughed and Ahaziah joined in.

Joash pushed back from his father's grasp at the sound of laughter and looked indignantly from Ahaziah to Sheba, as though to say *how dare you laugh at my tears.*

The King and the Princess burst into hysterics and the boy finally broke into a smile, giggling along with the merriment.

****

'You delivered the message?' Isaac flicked a coin to the barman and waited for the ale to appear on the long bar in front of him.

'I did.'

'How did he take it?'

'I gave it to an acolyte. I would have liked to have seen his face though.'

'You and me both. Have a drink and then you need to return to the valley with the others. Stay out of sight.'

'Yes Sir.' The soldier did not salute the assassin. Those who travelled with him knew he held no regard for the military he served. He was his own man for hire and Jehu was paying well.

The tall jugs of ale arrived and both men lifted them in unison, draining the contents quickly. 'I wish I had time to savour this, but duty calls.' Isaac placed the empty cup on the bar and turned. He saw a young, small robed figure by the door and nodded at his companion.

'Is that the acolyte from the temple?'

'It is.' The officer looked questioningly at his commander.

'You had better find out what he wants.'

The soldier drained the last of his ale and walked over to the boy whose nervous eyes were only slightly obscured by his hood. The acolyte handed him a piece of paper, which he took and nodded for the boy to leave. He wasted no time, running from the gaze of so many unsavoury patrons.

'What is it?' Isaac asked as the soldier arrived back by his side.

'A note for Jehu from the Priest it seems.'

'What does it say?'

'I did not read it. It is for the General, not me.' Isaac reached out and took the parchment from his hands. The soldier knew better than to protest. Instead, he took the opportunity to remove himself from the firing line. 'I will return to camp then. You can figure out what to do with that.' The man nodded to the now unrolled note in the assassin's hands.

Isaac only muttered an inaudible agreement as he read the note. *The marriage is strategic. Please, I beg of you. Trust me in this.*

'Interesting.' Isaac spoke aloud to no-one.

Chapter 16

Thaliah considered her plans carefully. She needed to convince Ahaziah to take the throne in Israel when the Zealots killed her brother, but she was not sure he would accept it.

He was always such a sensitive boy, but he was all that was left of her family line and the idea that they could rule over all of Israel and Judah would be the fruition of all that Thaliah had ever hoped for.

When her mother had allowed her to be married to the King of Judah, she had been horrified. Her father had given the orders of course, but she still blamed her mother. Yes, Jerom was kind. He treated her well and she became a Queen, but it was a lonely time in her life and she still bore the scars.

Her dependence on that damned concoction from the Baal priests had been her saving grace for many years now, but the more she used it, the more she knew she was not in control and she liked to be in control; of everything.

She took one last look in the mirror and applied some cream to try to cover the dark rings that were so obvious around her eyes. Her hair was pulled back in a long braid and she scowled at the grey hairs staring back at her in the mirror.

There was only one way to convince Ahaziah to take Jehoram's kingdom. Now, she would find out if it was going to work. She swung from the mirror and left her rooms.

On the way to Ahaziah, she stopped to ensure all the preparations were in place for the wedding. This union would tie her in to the temple of Yahweh and provide some sort of protection against the Zealots once Ahaziah took the throne of Israel. She would use Jehoiada to convince them that her father Ahab's line, those who worshipped Baal, were all gone.

She took a tour of the great hall, laid out with long tables covered with white linen tablecloths and large vases with purple, blue and white flowers. The walls were adorned with delicate silk ribbons and each join boasted a bunch of water lilies imported from Egypt just for the occasion.

The wedding would take place on the steps of the temple and she made a mental note to inspect the temple before tomorrow morning. Priests had a habit of being benign when it came to wedding decorations and she would ensure the temple looked perfect for the occasion.

If only she could manage to find a suitable bride for her son. Ahaziah still refused to marry, but at least he had a male heir now. Not all was lost. Joash would stay with her while her son established himself in Israel. She would teach him to be a strong king, like her Grandfather. Omir was respected throughout the Kingdom and reigned over Israel and Judah as one nation. She would once again join the two into one.

Ahaziah was occupied in his private chambers, a pile of scrolls covered his table and he was mulling over a map as the Queen-Mother joined him.

'My son. You are looking tired.' She smiled as she circled to the end of the long table, joining Ahaziah to peruse the maps and messages.

'Tomorrow will be a big day mother. I hope to get to bed early tonight. I have been busy planning how I can help Jehoram regain his strength and control of Israel.'

'Funny you should mention that. I was just thinking the exact same thing,'

'You were?' Ahaziah failed to keep the scepticism from his voice.

'Yes. Of course I was. My brother is said to be more unwell than we were led to believe.'

'Yes. I have been advised of the same, but how did you discover such news?' Ahaziah had ceased to read his map. Instead, he rolled it up and tied it securely with a leather binding. He surveyed his table to ensure no vital pieces of information were easily visible.

'I have my sources.' She was not about to tell him the Priest of Baal had shared such insights. He was so sensitive about her temple visits of late.

'I will leave the morning after tomorrow. Once I know Sheba is wed and settled.'

'She will be fine. The Priest is absolutely enamoured of her. He will take good care of her. Now to more pressing business. Your Uncle.'

'Yes. I will take my senior generals with me as discussed. We need to discover if there is any way we can regain control of Rashom and I am quite sure the Zealots are up to something.'

'Yes, about that.' Ahaziah had been watching his mother carefully. She shuffled scrolls as she walked around the table, something obviously on her mind.

'If your Uncle should fall, you must seize the throne of Israel my son.'

'Why on earth would Jehoram fall? He is wounded, not dying.'

'Yes, but there are rumours. I am sure you have heard them. If the Zealots do come against him, promise me you will seek refuge in the fortress. We can send more men and rout the faction. All you need to do is give yourself time.'

'You believe the Zealots mean to attack the King directly? Surely that is too brazen, even for them. And where would you get such information?'

'It is only a rumour. I am only saying that should this happen, save yourself Ahaziah. I will look after Judah, and you can rule in Israel. We can have the entire Kingdom; just promise me you will not do anything foolish.'

Ahaziah looked carefully at his mother's eyes. The dark rings were not hidden by her feeble attempts with creams and colours. There was something sinister lying below the surface that he could not read and he decided now was not the time to challenge her.

'Thank you for your counsel Mother. You are wise as always.' He smiled, hoping she would not push him any further.

Thaliah seemed to consider his words carefully before smiling and moving to the door. 'I must check on the wedding preparations. I will see you tomorrow.' She twirled around with uncharacteristic exuberance and almost danced from the room.

Ahaziah frowned at his mother's behaviour, before returning to the various reports still sprawled around his table.

Chapter 17

'Has he kept his word?' Sheba lunged at Aron with her sword, which he deflected before moving in with both a short sword and dagger drawn.

'Focus Sheba, now is not the time to check up on your future husband.'

Sheba ignored the comment, realising immediately that Aron was trying to distract her. He knew she was easily goaded when it came to Jehoiada. Instead, she blocked both weapons as they systematically tried to strike her, one after another. She was pushed back, but each blow was blocked by her own sword and dagger.

'Good, very good.' Aron encouraged. 'Just watch I do not box you in. The wall is only just behind you now. What are you planning to do?' Aron suddenly changed the rhythm of his advance, bringing both weapons to bear at the same time, one high toward Sheba's neck, the other, aimed at her thigh.

Sheba blocked the lower blow and ducked her head under the intended strike to her neck. Aron's balance faltered as the Princess side-stepped around him and rolled, coming to her feet in a smooth motion, a few paces to his rear.

The soldier swung around quickly, taking in Sheba's triumphant grin. 'Perfect! I did not even see that coming. Time to take a break. I am starving. How about you?'

Sheba kept smiling but did not lower her weapons. 'I am hungry, but I am also having a great deal of fun right now.'

'Alright. You tell me when you are ready.' Aron prepared for more sparring.

They trained until they were both dripping with sweat. The afternoon was growing cool, but they were oblivious to it.

'Alright, now I am hungry but I think I need to change before we get a meal.' The Princess sheathed her weapons and made her way to her rooms. They had spent the past few weeks training in every spare moment. When Sheba was not required at wedding rehearsals or fittings or menu meetings or some other useless task, she was hot and sweaty with Aron just as she was now.

'To answer your question.' Aron waited for the Princess to realise what he was talking about. He walked alongside, his bronze chest bare, with his tunic wrapped around his neck and only a pair of pants to his waist.

'Oh. I almost forgot. Yes, has my future husband stayed away from the Zealots?' Sheba tried to keep her eyes from Aron's sweaty chest, but it was growing more and more difficult. Her brother's words rang in her head as she tried to shake her desires free.

'As far as I can tell, yes. He has not met with anyone I recognise from the faction.'

'Damn!' They had reached her rooms and the Princess opened the door wide. 'You coming in?'

Aron hesitated for a moment. 'Damn what?'

Sheba smiled as she touched his bare chest with the tip of her finger. 'You will have to come in and find out.'

Aron looked over his shoulder. Since Sheba had told him what the King had said about the servants talking, he had tried to be more careful about not giving the wrong impression. But since then, the servants had made themselves scarce. Like today, there was no-one in the courtyard, so he joined the Princess.

'You are terrible Sheba. Damn what?' He asked as he closed the door behind him.

'Damn, because that means I have to go ahead with the marriage,' Sheba pouted. 'My brother told me something else when he told me to be careful.' She moved forward, her heart racing as she placed her palm in the middle of Aron's chest.

Her bodyguard did not say a word, his eyes told her everything she needed to know. 'He told me that I would have to make many sacrifices, but you were not one of them.' She put her arms around his neck and kissed his bottom lip. He did not move, so she kissed his top lip. He moaned slightly as he wrapped his arms around her waist and placed his lips over hers.

Sheba undid her scabbard, that dropped to the ground with a thud. Aron did the same, without taking his lips from hers. She undid her leather waist belt and threw it across the room. She tore her tunic over her head with so much haste, she caught her braid in the process.

They both giggled nervously before Aron lifted her from her feet and carried her to her bed. He laid her down more gently than she expected and hovered over her a moment. 'Are you sure?' She dragged his face to hers and kissed him with passion.

She could have spoken. She could have said of course she was. She could have screamed that she wanted him, not some old priest to be her first, but she did not need to. He untied the laces on his pants and she opened her legs for him.

'Not so fast Princess.' He smiled as he pulled back to take in the view of her naked body. He explored every spot with his lips, one piece at a time and Sheba moaned with growing passion.

Her body shook as her moans became louder and Aron finally silenced her with his lips once more. She wrapped her legs around him as they became one and for the first time in a very long time, she could think of nothing except the pleasure of being a young woman in love.

Chapter 18

Aron had waited all day it seemed to escort the Princess to the temple for her wedding. There was a piece of him that struggled now with her marriage, but he knew it had to go ahead.

She had lain in his arms for half the night before he had left for his own room. As he had walked away from her bed he had been torn. To be a consort to a Princess, who was married to a High priest with links to the zealot factions was dangerous, for both of them.

The King had convinced her that she was entitled and that her bodyguard would not see her stoned to death, but their world was changing, and if the faction gained traction, it would be a difficult task to keep her safe if they were discovered.

He was jolted out of his daydream as the door to the Princess's rooms opened. She was surrounded by servants who fussed over every detail of her dress, hair and make-up.

She made eye contact with him immediately, pleading for him to end her torment. He smiled at her discomfort, but as the servants began to move away, he struggled to keep his feelings from his face.

He shook himself and moved to take her arm. 'Give the Princess some space people. I will escort her to the King.'

This moment with her would not last long before Ahaziah took over and he wanted her all to himself. The servants scattered with mutters and minor indignation, but they liked the Princess's bodyguard. She had been an introverted and miserable girl before he came along.

They waited for the walkway to clear before slowly making their way to the King's courtyard. 'You look beautiful.' Aron smiled as he touched her hand.

'I feel like a peacock.' She looked up at Aron, but forced a smile she knew he needed to see. 'I am worried. Will Jehoiada know?'

Aron shook his head. 'No. He will have no idea. Contrary to common belief, a virgin does not always give a sign that she is a virgin. If you stay as nervous as you are now, he will have no idea.'

'Good.' She exhaled, trying to relax.

'Are you regretting it, us I mean?'

'Never. I told Jehoiada I would keep you with me after the wedding. You are mine Aron. I have already told you, before last night, you were always mine.' Sheba smiled, suddenly feeling more comfortable with what she had to do. 'Just remember, today is my duty, you are my chosen.'

Aron did not need the reassurance, but he appreciated it. He grinned mischievously. 'You may not see me at the wedding, but I will be watching your every move.'

'I believe you.' Sheba held his hand tighter as they reach Ahaziah's courtyard.

'Ah, there you are. Fashionably late of course.' The King had been pacing, but quickly composed himself and greeted his sister with a hug as Aron reluctantly let her hand go.

'Did you think I would not come?' The Princess grinned at her brother's concern. 'I had to endure the seamstress, the maids and a crazy looking man, with brightly coloured clothes who simply would not stop putting flowers in my braid.'

The King laughed heartily. 'He is Mother's friend. I have tried to decide if he is a man or a woman. He dresses like a man, but his manner is that of a fussing old maid.'

'That is him. He was very funny though. Kept grumbling at the maids about the colour of my eyes not suiting the colour of the powders they were using.'

'Come, it is time to take you to the temple. The Priest must be beside himself with worry by now.'

'He will have to learn to wait.' Sheba winked at Ahaziah who patted her hand as she took his arm.

'As it should be Sheba.'

Aron watched the Princess leave with the King. They were flanked by four of the King's personal guard, all armed, all big enough to take care of any threat.

He followed at a discreet distance. Today was not the day to be seen anywhere near Sheba. Today was the day to stand back and let all the attention fall on her and her husband-to-be. It was the safest option.

One of the soldiers helped the Princess into a carriage. The King stood alongside her and once she was settled, he flicked the reins for the two white Arabian horses to start their short journey to the temple.

The King's personal war chariot looked all the more glorious with the beautiful bride in her golden dress. Its bronze patterns of battles fought by King David and Solomon were fashioned around the top and the front embossed with the likeness of Solomon's temple, the same temple that they were riding to today. The carriage was nothing short of regal.

The temple was the only one in the whole of Israel and Judah. All other places of worship were traditional tabernacles, tents erected in various places as the need arose.

As the King's carriage approached the temple, Aron noticed a man standing by a stone pillar, just inside the first courtyard. He slowed his pace and moved to the side, stopping behind one of the tall palm trees that lined the avenue.

There was something about the way the man stood. He was a military man, and well trained by the look of it. He was not hiding, but he was trying not to be seen. Aron moved between the palm trees as all attention fell on the Princess and the King, riding through the heavy stone archway that separated the temple from the cobbled avenue that led from the palace.

As the carriage passed, the man moved into the shadows and disappeared. Aron moved quickly to catch up with the Princess. The heckles on the back of his neck were raised and in the back of his mind, he was sure he had seen this man before.

As he entered the temple grounds, a hand touched his shoulder. He turned with his sword drawn in one fluid motion. 'Aron. Is that you?'

Aron dropped his sword arm. 'Isaac?'

'The one and only, brother. I had no idea you were in Jerusalem! How long have you been here?'

'Close to a month now. I was sent by the King.' Aron sheathed his weapon.

'Ah. I might have known he would send you as his envoy. It seems this little Swaraj has held up the proceedings.'

'Yes, it does look that way.' Aron knew there was only one reason why Isaac was here and he had no intention of giving away more details about his own mission.

'Pretty girl. The Priest is very lucky.' Isaac grinned, but it failed to reach his eyes. 'So why are you still here? Surely you had to deliver a message and then be on your way?' Isaac's question was casual, but Aron knew his brother never missed a detail in anything he saw or heard.

'More to the point Isaac, what are you doing here? No offence, but wherever you go, death follows.'

'True, true enough. I have no immediate orders.'

'Immediate?'

'Immediate.'

Aron watched the chariot move into the main courtyard, which was full of guests all clamouring for a glimpse of the beautiful Princess.

'Looks like we might miss the fun if we do not catch up.' Isaac watched his brother's gaze as he spoke. 'You know the Princess?'

Aron realised he had allowed his attention to wander for a moment too long. 'I do. I am her bodyguard.' He had considered keeping the truth from Isaac, but if Sheba were his target, he would know soon enough.

'That is a nice work detail. Why I cannot snag one like that I am not sure.'

'We both know why brother. Guarding is not exactly your forté now is it?' Aron's words held no malice.

When they had joined the army, they had both been very young, hungry and desperate to belong to something. Isaac had always been willing to do anything to feed himself—steal, cheat, even kill. Aron had been more persuasive, controlled and calculated. Either way, they had both become who they were and there was no going back now.

Aron decided to make himself clear. 'I hope you are not here for her or her brother, Isaac. I would hate to have to come against you, but you know I will if I have to.'

Isaac slapped him casually on the shoulder. 'I have no desire to kill you brother, but an assignment is an assignment.'

'Yes, but one of us follows our orders out of duty, the other for gold.'

'There is that.'

'Is it worth it?'

'What?'

'Is the gold worth your soul?'

'I lost my soul a long time ago Aron. The gold is all I have left.'

'No, you still have me. You have always had me brother.'

Isaac's eyes softened for only a moment before he put his barrier back in place. 'We have work to do. Your Princess is getting out of sight brother.'

Aron looked over at the carriage and nodded. 'She is never out of my sight Isaac, never!' He moved off toward the entrance of the temple. He watched the King escort Sheba up the temple steps.

The large, curved entrance, with enormously tall pillars provided shade for the bride and her honoured guests, while all others stood below, in the courtyard.

He could feel Isaac's eyes on him as he took the stairs to the side entrance into the Priest's private rooms. He knew they adjoined the inside of the temple and eventhough the area was sacred, used only by the Priests, he did not care. He needed to be as close as possible to Sheba.

As he took the stairs to the vestibule, he could hear the ceremony had already started. He reached the top of the spiral staircase and waited beyond the doorway that led from the Priest's robe room to the vestibule. The curtain that covered the entrance was too thick to see through, so he moved it slightly, making a tiny viewing point so he could watch over the Princess throughout the ceremony.

As the Priest wrapped Sheba's hand with Jehoiada's, Aron's heart raced. He forced himself to remain still. There was no way he could stop the proceedings. The Princess had to marry the Priest. Jezebel had assured him that this part of the vision was unambiguous.

As Jehoiada moved to kiss his bride, Sheba physically flinched, but closed her eyes and accepted the sealing of her future with the grace and dignity Aron had come to expect.

Chapter 19

Sheba sat to the left of the King, with Jehoiada by her side. The Queen-Mother occupied the King's right side at the head of the great hall.

Alongside the bridal table, a band of musicians played accompanying music as the sound of revelry grew louder with more wine that was consumed.

Aron had waited most of the night, but he needed to warn Ahaziah that an assassin was in Jerusalem. He moved forward and bowed to the King. He dropped his head between Sheba and Ahaziah to whisper in the King's ear. The smell of lotus flower drifted to his senses, almost creating goose bumps on his skin.

'Your Grace. I need to speak with you a moment. It is a matter of urgency. Please, forgive the intrusion.'

Ahaziah looked at Aron's face and nodded. He could not leave the table. It would signify an end to the festivities. Instead, he turned to face the bodyguard and indicated for him to move closer.

Aron dropped to his haunches as the King moved his head to listen. 'I have seen a man who is a known assassin for General Jehu. He is in Jerusalem and is watching Sheba's wedding.'

The King raised an eyebrow. 'Fetch the Captain of the guard for me Aron. Advise him of what you have seen. Describe the man and make sure his men keep an eye out. I will meet with you as soon as the feast is over.'

'Thank you.' Aron nodded to the King as he rose, acknowledging Sheba with a wink. 'It is nothing to worry about Princess.'

Sheba said nothing, but she could tell Aron was worried. She had strained to hear his conversation with her brother, but she had only caught a few words.

'You should not eavesdrop on the matters of men Sheba.' Her husband patted her hand as he spoke.

It took all her control to not respond verbally, but she moved her hand away from Jehoiada's and firmly entwined it with her other in her lap where he could not reach it with any sort of public decency.

He looked at her with a puzzled expression and she returned his gaze with obvious disdain. Jehoiada reached for his wine and swallowed a large mouthful, before studying the cup and deciding to drink the rest to calm his nerves.

The Princess smiled at his action and hoped in the back of her mind that he would be too drunk to perform his marital duties, but she was relatively positive that would not be the case.

****

The King finally called an end to the evening, against Sheba's constant begging of him not to. The couple left the table with the King amongst an escort of no less than ten armed guards.

'Take the Princess and her husband to her rooms. They will spend the night in the palace.' The Captain of the guard saluted and passed orders to four guards, who flanked Sheba and Jehoiada as they left.

Aron watched the Priest stumble and smiled as the Princess made no attempt to hinder his fall.

'That poor man has no idea what he has gotten himself into.' Ahaziah spoke quietly to Aron as they made their way to his private chambers, flanked by the remaining six guards.

'You have stationed a guard outside her rooms?'

'Of course, until you return to take his place.' Ahaziah winked and Aron frowned. 'Do not worry yourself man. Your secret is more than safe with me.'

Aron nodded and refocussed. 'The man I saw your Grace is a paid assassin, a mercenary of sorts. He wears the uniform of a King's Officer but make no mistake, he is in the employ of Jehu.'

'How do you know this?' Two guards took their post outside the atrium that led to the King's wing, as the remaining entourage continued down the corridor.

'He is well known to me.' Two more guards stopped, turned to face outwards and stood at attention as the two men moved into the corridor leading to Ahaziah's private chambers.

'Really, how so?' The King studied Aron who seemed reluctant to elaborate, until they reached the end of the corridor. He stopped and opened the door to his room as the remaining two guards took their post outside the door. The King closed the door behind them and waited expectantly for Aron to continue.

'He is my brother.' Aron stood waiting for the barrage of questions that was bound to come.

'Your brother? Good lord Aron. Your brother is an assassin?'

'I am afraid so. I am only thankful I was here to recognise him. We spoke briefly.'

'You spoke with him?' The King's eyes grew wider as he bolted the door closed.

'Yes your Grace. He said he was not under any specific orders yet, but I think he has a target. He just has not been given the final order.'

'Disturbing. How am I to leave Jerusalem now?'

'You could be the target your Grace. He will follow you if you are. I suggest you double your private guards'

'And if I am not the target?'

'If he does not follow you, then I will know it is either Sheba, the Priest or your mother.'

'You cannot possibly protect them all Aron.'

'I have no intention of protecting them all. I will however coordinate with the Captain of the guard to protect your mother. The Priest I honestly do not care one way or the other about. He is still in league with the Zealots. Or if he has, as Sheba ordered him, cut all ties, he may well be the target for that reason. My focus is purely on Sheba.'

'I am sure it is.' Ahaziah grinned but stilled Aron as he made to protest. 'I am jesting man. You had better get a thicker skin if you intend to keep your affair private.'

Aron nodded his understanding and smiled. 'Your sister will be the death of me your Grace.'

'Of that I have no doubt.'

Chapter 20

Sheba need not have worried about Jehoiada. The man was drunk, obviously inexperienced and the act was over in the blink of an eye.

She rose from the bed, collecting her robe to cover her night dress and quietly opened the front door of her rooms.

The guard on duty snapped to attention and the Princess shushed him reflexively. The last thing she needed right now was for Jehoiada to wake up.

'Take a seat. There is no need to follow me. I will only be in the garden, enjoying the full moonlight.'

The guard looked sheepishly at the Princess and made to follow her in any case, but she pointed to the stone bench by the door and frowned at him until he succumbed to the pressure.

The Princess felt the chill of the season changing and gathered her robe tightly in one hand, as she touched the jasmine flowers on the side of the path with the other hand. The scent wafted into the still evening, filling her with a sudden sense of melancholy.

She found a spot of grass and sat down in the middle of the light from the moon, ignoring the moisture from the already dew-covered ground. 'I feel like a prize bull, sold to the highest bidder.' She spoke aloud to no-one in particular.

'You are nothing of the sort my child.' The Princess turned to the voice, trying to focus on the transparent form before her.

'Asherah?'

'Yes. I felt your sorrow.'

'You can feel that,' she pointed to the star filled night sky, 'from all the way up there?'

The Goddess chuckled softly and the sound drifted in the still air like wind chimes. 'It is hard sometimes to tune out the emotions of those you are concerned for.'

'Concerned for me? Why?'

'Because you chose to follow your destiny and it will not be an easy path to follow.'

'Now you tell me.' The Princess smiled as Asherah's image became more solid and the Goddess touched her shoulder affectionately.

'You have made the right choice, but when the time comes and you need me, really need me, just call my name and I will answer you.'

'You are not going to explain, are you?'

'I am afraid I cannot.'

'I know, free will and all that. Yahweh has a lot to answer for you know.'

'To Him, your life is but a blink of His eye. That does not mean you are not important, but He sees everyone; the past, the present and the future and He knows the outcome.'

'Then what would have happened if I had not followed this all-important destiny of mine?'

'Then He would have found another way.'

'This is all too much for a simple Princess to comprehend. I am tired Asherah. It has been a long day and I am lonely already, even after such festivities.'

The Goddess reached out once more and touched her finger to Sheba's brow. The Princess felt the tingle between her eyes and smiled as the feeling of serenity surrounded her.

'Sleep well child.' Asherah vanished as the Princess walked back to her rooms.

The guard looked at her as though she had gone quite mad, for as he had watched her, he had seen only the Princess, talking to the sky.

****

Asherah ascended through the veil that separated humans from the divine. She had not returned to her sisters for quite some time and something was niggling at the back of her mind.

Moloch had been quite brazen in his manipulation of recent events and she was at a loss to see what his motive might be. He had no interest in boosting Baal's earthly horde, yet he played his games with Thaliah, but to what end?

The woman was unstable, but she was never going to break the line of the Redeemer. She was intent on seeing her line rule over all of Israel. It had been her only thought whenever the Goddess had listened in on her somewhat crazed mind.

The Zealots thought they were doing the right thing, but even Elijah had not been arrogant enough to think he could choose who ruled over Judah and Israel.

Yes, he had killed the Priests of Baal, much to Asherah's disdain, but he had never once tried to interfere with who Yahweh saw fit to rule His land.

Why was the young prophet Elisha leading this revolt? She needed to enlist help from her sisters to discover what was really going on, before it was too late.

The Goddess took a deep breath, eventhough air was unnecessary, the action relaxed her nerves. As she entered the Holy realm, the brilliant lights that made vision impossible for humanity, only highlighted the beauty for Asherah.

The Heavens were an image of what her Father had wanted for the world below. Every corner was full of lush plants bearing fruit that never aged. Each piece was perfect in size, shape and colour and Asherah smiled at the knowledge that not a piece would ever be eaten by the Angels, for they had no need of food.

The rolling hills, that surrounded her Father's home were blue with tinges of grey and covered in snow, that never melted. Waterfalls cascaded from all four corners of the sanctuary and it reminded the Goddess of her own such place above Jericho—before the fall—when her people were still free to worship nature and all it provided.

She found Astarte and Anath duelling in a large clearing of green velvet soft grass and stopped to watch them.

Anath's glowing sword sang as it moved effortlessly through the air. Astarte blocked every blow with her golden staff, a weapon Asherah had not seen before. With every strike between the weapons, sparks of light danced.

'We are almost done Asherah.' Astarte spoke without looking at her sister.

'Who is winning?' Asherah asked, knowing neither would concede.

'I am.' They both answered in unison and Asherah laughed, the sound louder and more fervent than she had intended.

Both women stopped. Astarte put her free hand on her hip, planting the staff into the soft ground indignantly, while Anath did the same with her sword, until it sank into the ground and she toppled sideways.

All three women exploded into a fit of laughter, while Astarte helped Anath back to her feet between giggles.

'Oh I have missed you two.' Asherah moved to her sisters and hugged them both, one in each arm.

'Where have you been this time?' Astarte struggled to speak without finding a mouthful of Asherah's hair in her face. Asherah finally let them both go.

'I have been trying to work out what Moloch is up to.'

'Oh Asherah, why can you not just spar with us, enjoy your life without being so worried about what our wayward brother is up to?'

'I wish I could, honestly I do, but it is not within me to turn a blind eye. Admit it, when I discover any of Moloch's schemes you both revel in the adventure to help me put a stop to it.' Asherah challenged amiably and her sisters exchanged knowing looks.

'See. I knew it.'

'Alright, alright, what is he up to this time?' Anath sheathed her sword and both Goddesses sat down on the grass, legs crossed. 'Do not just stand there. Take a seat. We have been training all morning and need a rest.'

Asherah joined her sisters on the soft carpet of grass and marvelled at the scent that wafted into the air as the blades crushed beneath her feet. She laughed, knowing it was only her imagination, for they were weightless in their own home realm and the grass would not even know they were there, if it were real, and they all knew it was not.

'I cannot be sure, but he has been spending time in Baal's temple in Judah. He has some sort of influence over Thaliah the Queen-Mother there, but I am at a loss to figure out what he hopes to gain.'

'Power I bet.' Anath looked to her sisters for confirmation.

'Him or the Queen-Mother?' Astarte challenged.

'Likely they both seek power. That is nothing new, but how does helping Thaliah, aid Moloch's cause?' Asherah continued.

'Well, if Baal's following grows through Thaliah, Moloch will have more allies.' Anath offered her opinion, knowing her sisters would likely disregard it. She was known for her warrior skills, not her strategy skills.

'Yes, but Thaliah does not openly worship Baal and she aligns herself with the Zealots through the Priest Jehoiada.'

'So what do the Zealots want?'

Asherah thought about it a moment. 'They want to kill anyone who does not follow Father.'

'Exactly!' Anath smiled triumphantly, as though the entire issue was resolved.

'Yes, they make no secret of it but that hardly answers the question of how Moloch hopes to stop the line of the Redeemer through aiding Thaliah.' Asherah frowned at Anath but directed her question to Astarte.

'Who carries the line?' Astarte asked, while tying her long black hair back into a braid, suddenly deciding this matter might be intriguing after all.

'Thaliah's son Ahaziah.'

'Alright, so the Zealots need to stop the worshiping of Baal, other than killing Baal priests, burning the temple and such, how else would they do so?'

'I thought we were talking about Moloch killing off the Redeemer's line.' Anath looked from Asherah to Astarte with a growing crease on her brow.

'Follow me on this sisters.' Astarte carried on with growing excitement. 'The Zealots and Moloch want the same outcome. Baal does not, but Baal has never been too bright if you ask me.'

Asherah's eyes opened widely. 'They both want to kill the King, or should I say Kings. Oh my goodness. Both Jehoram and Ahaziah have allowed free religion in Judah and Israel and the Zealots can stop that, if they kill them and Moloch will get what he wants. But only if the children all die, will the line die with them.'

'Exactly.' Astarte smiled triumphantly.

Asherah's vision suddenly made more sense. Unlike Yahweh, she could not see the entire future, just pieces of it. 'I knew Thaliah was a threat to Sheba and I knew the Princess would have to choose, but I had no idea why! Thaliah could end the line of the Redeemer.'

'Why would Thaliah kill her son's children, just because her son dies?' Anath looked positively baffled by Asherah's revelation.

'I believe that is where our lovely brother has come into the picture.' Astarte scowled at the thought.

'What are we going to do?' Anath stood up and drew her weapon in one fluid motion.

'Sit down Anath. All that I do has been to stop the war that we know is coming to the Eternal Realm, not start it.'

Asherah thought about Gabriel's words. 'We have to fight this with love, not hate Anath.'

'I am good at love.' Anath grinned mischievously.

'Not that kind of love sister.' Astarte pushed Anath in the shoulder and they both laughed.

Chapter 21

Sheba held Joash on her hip and helped him wave goodbye to his father. Aron stood at her side, watching with eagle eyes, anyone who moved around the main courtyard or surrounding long verandas that flowed from the barracks, to the palace and beyond.

'What are you looking for?' She whispered.

'I will explain later.'

'Is this why I had a poor wide-eyed, bored guard sitting outside my door all last night? I heard you talking to Ahaziah, but you two could have had the decency to explain to *me* what was going on.'

'I just said I would explain did I not?' Aron gave her a warning look she had not seen before. 'Now is not the time.'

'It is time for some food now is it not little man? Let us go find you some food.' Sheba moved her attention to her nephew who giggled at her overly exaggerated tone.

'I will come with you.' Aron followed the Princess, his eyes still darting around the compound like wildfire.

'Very well.' Sheba spoke formally, trying to keep up all sense of propriety in public. She continued to carry Joash until they reached the stairs to the palace. The rough stones on the courtyard were fine for horses and sandals, but not for soft little feet like his.

As she popped him down, she ruffled his curly black hair with her fingers. 'Off to Dada's house. I will follow you. You show me the way.' She smiled as his eyes lit up with excitement.

He toddled in front of her, while she waited for Aron to catch up. 'Now can we talk?'

'When we reach Ahaziah's wing. I suggest we eat in the courtyard.'

'That is a fine idea.' She spoke formally and louder in case of onlookers.

'You might be overdoing it a little.' Aron whispered as soon as they were out of view.

'I am sorry. I am just a little jittery and you hunting every dark corner like a poacher is not helping one little bit.' She reached down to take Joash's hand as he held it up for her.

'He is adorable.' Aron smiled at the little boy's dimples.

'He most certainly is. He will miss his father. They are inseparable for the most part.'

'He adores the boy; that is obvious.'

'You know he made Jehoiada swear to protect him before he would let him marry me.' Sheba laughed.

'Is that what Jehoiada told you?'

'Heavens no. Ahaziah did. He told me that my marriage was conditional on three things—my happiness, Joash's protection and the Queen-Mother's impotence.'

'Now that is precious. She obviously did not know anything about that.'

They had reached the King's wing which was once again quiet and free of guards. There were very few servants present, except those who were busy cleaning and fussing over the King's garden.

They walked into the large circular atrium with coloured tiles on the floor and doors leading in all directions. Aron knew one went to the long corridor that led to the King's private chambers. Another led to the courtyard where he had trained with Sheba, but there were two more and curiosity was now overwhelming him.

'Where do the two other archways lead?'

'One is used by the servants. There are little passageways that lead off in various directions including the store room, the cookhouse and the great hall. Ahaziah uses it when he wants to discreetly make his way around the palace.'

'And the other?'

'The treasury and throne room. Ahaziah hates the throne room. It is too formal, but he likes the treasury room.' Sheba smiled. 'Who would not?'

'Indeed.'

The Princess found Joash's nursemaid in Ahaziah's rooms and sent her to find them all food. The toddler was getting tired of walking and lifted his arms to his aunt, who collected him up and hugged him, tickling his tummy as his father so often did.

They went through Ahaziah's expansive apartment and sat down in the courtyard. Joash played on the grass while they waited for the meal to arrive.

'Is it later enough?' Sheba grinned as Aron looked around the courtyard ensuring no-one would overhear them.

'I saw someone yesterday who poses a threat.'

'That part was fairly obvious by all the guards wandering around most of the night. A little more detail could prove advantageous.' The Princess tried unsuccessfully to keep the sarcasm from her voice.

'Alright. There is an assassin in Jerusalem. Almost certainly in the employ of the Zealot faction.'

'And how do you know this?'

'I saw him. I spoke to him. I know him. I explained all this to your brother.'

'Yes but I was not there, remember!'

Aron stopped himself. He took a deep breath. He knew he was not handling this well. 'I know this because he is my brother.'

Sheba heard the shame in his voice and placed her hand on his. Aron looked up, not at her, but around the courtyard once more, hoping no-one had seen.

'You are being paranoid. I am sure the assassin will not make it into the King's own private wing.'

'It is not that. I am just being cautious about *us*.'

'Oh.' Sheba look her hand away from Aron's suddenly realising he could be right.

'This is going to be harder than I thought.' Sheba slumped back into the soft cushions and pouted.

Chapter 22

Isaac watched the King's entourage leave the palace main courtyard. He knew Aron would be watching for him, but he had many years of experience in his craft and was not about to watch in plain sight.

Security had been tightened since he had spoken with Aron. There was no way anyone who was not known to the Captain of the guard was going to set one foot inside the palace walls, even the main courtyard, without being noticed.

What the Captain had not thought about, was removing carts, market stalls and the many objects that made scaling the outer wall all too easy for someone like Isaac.

He smiled as he thought about how easy it had been to offer the merchant a gold coin in exchange for access. The man had been dubious at first, but when Isaac explained that his brother was a very important man inside the palace and he just had to see how he was, the merchant was most obliging.

Now, as he watched Aron moving away from the courtyard, the Princess and her nephew under his care, it was obvious where his brother's loyalties lay. The touch of her elbow to escort her spoke volumes. A guard, touching a Princess; they were very familiar with one another.

His orders still had not been clarified and Isaac was torn. He took the note from his pocket and read it once more. *The marriage is strategic. Please, I beg of you. Trust me in this.*

He knew he had broken Aron's heart when he had been chosen to train as an assassin. Was he willing to break it again? He looked at the note once more and without thinking any further and before he could change his mind, he tore it to small pieces. This was one thing Jehu did not need to know.

****

Moloch hovered unseen above the palace, trying to read the assassin. It was usually a very simple task, but Isaac was different. Most assassins enjoyed the hunt, the kill, but Isaac was unusual. For him, it was just a job, a means to riches and nothing more.

Angels could not so much listen to human thoughts, as feel their emotions and see the ever-changing colours of their aura. Usually Moloch could read almost anyone with even the smallest amount of darkness in their soul, but not this time.

How was he to manipulate someone who did not follow conventional order? Moloch shook his head. The man was a paid assassin, when the time came, he would take the kill shot so what was he so worried about?

'Interesting fellow that one.' Moloch swung to see Anath behind him. His sisters rarely snuck up on him, but Anath was different. They had been very close once, but that time had passed.

'Since when did you start sneaking around and spying on me?' There was no malice in his voice as he raised a questioning eyebrow.

'Oh you look so cute when you do that.' Anath casually came closer to Moloch, patting his cheek as she used to.

Moloch knew then that she must be helping Asherah once more. 'You are doing Asherah's bidding again I see.'

'Bidding no, just a favour. She asked me to keep an eye on you. You have been quite busy it seems. Like I said, he is a hard one to gauge.'

Anath returned her gaze to the assassin who was now returning to the street where he had scaled the wall.

'What do you want with him?' The Goddess remained casual, as though Moloch had nothing better to do than answer her questions. She smiled as he grew tense.

'You know I am just trying to restore us Anath?'

Moloch had explained his reasoning to his closest confidante many times before and for so many years, Anath had followed him, believed in him, but the battle of Jericho had changed all that. His willingness to destroy thousands of lives for his cause had been too much.

'We do not need restoration brother. We live in harmony, in the heavens with our Father. We are supposed to watch over the humans for Him, not destroy them.

'I have no desire to watch the humans.'

'Yet you do, all the time, just maliciously, not respectfully as we are instructed.'

'You had followed me once.'

'I was a jealous fool once. Humanity is innocent Moloch. You cannot blame them for the choices Father makes. If you continue to try to make war on them, there will be a war between all our brethren and no-one really wants that. You stopped Dagon when we were in danger. I know you do not want that.'

'If the Redeemer does not come, they will never know peace.' Moloch cast his arm around the world below him. 'They will destroy each other and we will once again be Father's focus.'

'You really never did understand brother. We were created to care for them, not instead of them. If you destroy humanity, Father will just start over, as He did after the fall and the floods.'

'Maybe He will not. After another failure, maybe He will finally be content with us.'

'Oh brother. You never were very good at sharing.' Anath smiled sympathetically before disappearing.

Moloch watched her go and frowned. 'We should not have to share.'

Chapter 23

Ahaziah had pushed his men and their mounts. He knew Jehoram needed him in Jezreel as soon as possible. It was late on the second day when his company of over a hundred of his most loyal men rode into the courtyard of Ahab's Fortress.

His Grandfather had built the fortress to house his cavalrymen and supplies for his many campaigns. The walls were too high and too straight to scale.

His hundred men nearly filled the courtyard to capacity as the King of Judah rode his mount to the steps leading to the fortress entrance. A soldier saluted him and took the reins as he dismounted.

'The King is expecting you your Grace.'

It had been years since Ahaziah had walked the halls of the small fortress, but he knew the way well. Without an escort, he entered the large archway leading to a small inner courtyard. From there, he took the short staircase to the battlements that surrounded the inner wall of the fortress.

The King was in the main common room, sitting at a table set above the surrounding long tables, flanked on each side with heavy wooden benches.

Ahaziah jumped the two steps to the dais and greeted his uncle, who did not move from his chair. His face was pale and sweat beaded on his brow.

'Jehoram, I would have come more quickly. I am sorry. I did not know how serious your wounds were and with Sheba's wedding...' He stopped apologizing and sighed.

'It is not your fault Ahaziah. I have kept my condition quiet for fear Jehu would storm the fortress if he knew. Aron knew I was injured, but I have grown worse over the past few weeks, not better as I had hoped.'

'What is going on?' Ahaziah sat down as his grandmother entered the room. He stood once more and she waved him back to his chair with a smile he had not realised he had missed.

'Grandmother. You look as beautiful as ever.'

'And you lie as well as always Ahaziah.' They exchanged a quick hug before Jezebel took a seat and they both returned their attention to Jehoram.

'That traitor Jehu is what is happening.' His grandmother answered the question before the King could.

'We do not know he is a traitor Mother.'

'He sides with the Zealots. That makes him a traitor.'

'Do not mind your grandmother Ahaziah. Her history with the Zealots is long and painful.'

'As is mine uncle. They nearly killed my entire family.'

'Of course. I understand the animosity but they are not *all* bad.'

'You always did believe the best of everyone Jehoram.' Jezebel touched his arm gently as the King took a ragged breath.

'We knew Jehu was planning something uncle, and we knew it was with the Zealots, but it is still unclear exactly what.'

'He plans to assassinate me. I called you here so I could ask you to take my mother away, before it is too late. She would not leave me here.'

'And neither will I.'

'See, I told you. A true child of Omri's line.' Jezebel smiled smugly.

'You are not being brave; you are being reckless. Both of you.' Jehoram protested between coughs.

'Do you know what my mother wanted me to do? She said if you were to die, I was to take your throne.'

Jezebel's mouth dropped open and Jehoram laughed, choking in the process.

'That daughter of mine. I saw a vision you know. Did Aron arrive? Is Sheba alright?'

'Mother, not that again?' Jehoram sighed, visibly fatigued by his injuries, but more so by his mother's visions it seemed.

'Yes, Aron arrived and there is an assassin in Jerusalem. He is one of Jehu's men.'

'Then what are you doing here?' Jezebel was on her feet now. 'Get back and protect your sister and your son.'

'Aron is looking after her Grandmother and her marriage to Jehoiada will secure her safety with the Zealots, at least we hope it does. We have done all we can. The rest is with Yahweh.'

'Yahweh, what has He ever done for me?' Jezebel snarled.

'More than you could possibly know.' Jehoram touched his mother's arm and pulled her back to her seat gently. 'Jehu has called me out to a meeting, on the battlefield of Ramoth. It seems he is unhappy with how the battle progressed and feels I might be to blame.'

'He has no right to judge his King.' Jezebel was indignant.

'I will come with you.' Ahaziah rose to prepare his men.

'No nephew. Stay here.' The King rose from his seat and walked slowly to the window that overlooked the courtyard below. He leant on the window sill, visibly worn by the short walk and took ragged breaths.

'If you are both too stubborn to leave as I request, then you need to prepare your men and guard my mother. Jehu has a following, but it should not be enough to overthrow your men and I have given my Captain of the guard orders to return to protect the fortress should anything happen to me.'

'You do not have to meet him.' Jezebel begged, as she joined her son. 'Let us just ride from here and return to Samaria. He will have no chance of causing us grief once we are home.'

'Mother,' Jehoram placed his hand gently on his mother's cheek. If my time is done, then no matter where I go, death will follow. Poison, ambush, there are so many ways of killing a king.'

Jezebel sniffed slightly, took her son's hand and kissed it. 'Very well. We will stay here. When will you meet with Jehu?'

'Tomorrow morning. I sent word as soon as I knew Ahaziah was due to arrive.'

 **Chapter 24**

'I do not like this Sheba. It is hard enough protecting you inside the palace walls, out here in the market place is almost impossible.'

The Princess smiled at her bodyguard and continued to make her selection from the spice merchant who was overjoyed to be serving the Princess.

'Why on earth would *I* be the target?'

'I cannot say. We are talking about religion and politics, anything is possible. What I do know is that if Isaac did not follow your brother, you could still be in danger.'

Isaac smiled as he approached his brother, who continued to scan the alleyways and market stalls like a hawk. His back was to the assassin, but Isaac knew he could turn in his direction at any moment.

He stepped into a side alley, just as Aron turned around. The assassin smiled to himself as the thrill of adrenalin surged in his veins.

He watched the couple closely, gauging if his first instincts were indeed correct. The Princess's smile was lively and genuine whenever they spoke and she continued to allow Aron to take her arm, rather than stay a discreet distance behind her.

The King had left. His orders would come soon he knew and for the first time in nearly ten years, Isaac was not looking forward to following them.

The couple left the marketplace through an alleyway which did not return to the palace. The assassin followed.

****

'Where are you going now?' Aron protested as Sheba skipped into a narrow, darkened alleyway that led into the residential area.

'Just follow me and you will find out.' Sheba wrapped her hijab around her face to cover all but her eyes and pulled Aron along with her.

'I hardly think this is a good idea Sheba.' Aron protested, pulling back on her arm, suddenly feeling uncomfortable.

The Princess stopped, her one arm full of fresh fruit and spices prevented her from putting both hands on her hips, but her posture was defiant.

'Look!' She began and Aron raised an eyebrow as she moved very close to him and continued in a whisper. 'I am married now. Like it or not, my room will not be accessible

for our rendezvous and of course, neither will
the temple apartments, so…'

She left the rest unsaid as though he
should obviously understand what she meant.

'Oh for the love of Yahweh. So, I have
made an arrangement in a less honest part of
town, where money buys secrets. Follow me
and just play along.'

'Play along with what?' Aron frowned.

'Just play along. I will explain soon.'
Sheba looped her arm in his once more and
pulled him down the alleyway. They passed
through tiny walkways only one person wide.
They were lined with steps leading up to small
doors and porches covered in potted herbs and
flowers. A cat sunned itself on the bottom step
of one such home and barely batted an eyelid as
the couple slipped by.

The alleyway took so many twists and
turns that Aron was most certainly lost. He tried
to keep his bearings but the little homes all
looked so similar except for the occasional
different coloured door. They passed under an
archway, where a flat stone wall rose at least
two storeys high.

The streets had become dirty and the pots
on the porches now only bore dead and wilted
plants too dry to recognise. A small boy tugged
on the Princess's fine robe as she passed and

when she looked at him, his eyes begged her for a coin.

Aron pushed her on, knowing that if she gave even one coin, they would have a parade of beggars chasing them through the alleyways.

They reached an intersection where the alleys parted left and right. There was a red door before them, with a plump woman smoking a hookah pipe on the doorstep. She smiled through blackened teeth and held out her hand.

Aron puzzled over the exchange as the Princess placed a silver coin in her palm and the woman nodded for her to proceed.

Sheba pulled Aron along behind her as they made their way into the dark passageway of the building. The ceilings were so low Aron had to duck to walk around. The Princess followed a hallway to the end where an open door welcomed them inside.

She pushed the door closed behind them and placed her purchases on a washstand with a badly mottled bronze mirror perched precariously on top. Aron fidgeted as he scanned the room. There was a small, untidy bed against a stone wall, with a makeshift side table made from an old stool, one leg of which was shorter than the other two. It rocked as Aron walked around the raised wooden floor.

'Sheba, you cannot be serious?'

'I want to be with you Aron. This was the best I could manage.' The Princess pouted as she now studied the room more closely.

'Yes, but this is a hovel. Something not even fit for a...'

'Whore.' Sheba finished for him. 'It is our only choice. We cannot find privacy anywhere else.'

Aron moved forward and took Sheba in his arms. 'I love you, you know that, but I will not take you to that bed.' He pointed to the dishevelled, straw filled mattress behind him. 'You could catch something from it and then how would you explain that to your husband, or the Queen-Mother?'

Sheba dropped her head to his chest and returned his embrace. She looked up into his eyes and kissed his lips, gently sucking on his bottom lip. 'We do not have to use the bed.' She breathed the words seductively before returning her lips to his.

Aron moaned as he gripped her buttocks and lifted her onto the wash stand, spilling lemons and herbs to the floor.

Chapter 25

Jehu waited on the field of Ramoth, where not so long ago he had lost too many men to count. Their blood still stained the ground where he stood and eventhough the fall of the rains after summer would grow the field poppies to cover them, he would not soon forget.

The General watched the King's entourage ride down the slope toward the plain below. His Captain remained behind, with a small group of soldiers, while the King pranced forward on his white stallion. The animal was uncannily tall, not desert bred, of that the General was sure.

Both men dismounted and let their horses crop the few blades of grass while they moved toward one another.

Jehu made no attempt to salute or bow before his King, not that Jehoram was surprised. The man had been less than loyal for some time and now Ahaziah had provided proof he was in league with the Zealots.

Neither man spoke for a moment, until Jehoram broke the silence. 'You wished to speak with me. Why here?'

'Look around you!' Jehu offered no further explanation.

'I have no need to look around Jehu. I was here during the battle. I recall clearly what it looks like. Try not to waste our time. What is it you want?'

'Do you not see the blood of your soldiers, the blood of your people?'

'War is not pretty General. If you do not have the stomach for it, might you look for another profession?' The King kept his eyes fixed on Jehu. He watched the General's clenched jaw twitching with barely contained rage.

'This is all your fault.'

'How is that possible? I fought with my men. I was wounded with them.'

'You allow your mother to worship Baal. We will never have Yahweh's favour while she continues to grow the heathen god's followers.'

'You really believe that Yahweh needs us to fight His battles? How little do you understand the power He wields.'

'He offers favour to those who worship Him and only Him.'

'No, He offers favour when He chooses, to whom He chooses. The Arameans are more powerful than us. They have more men. They fight with strategies we are yet to understand.

Yahweh has nothing to do with this fight. He likely cares nothing for the feud of warring nations over land and resources.'

'We will never know peace as long as all this witchcraft and idolatry occurs. This is why he does not grant us victory. It is your fault.'

'You make no sense Jehu. I know you are aligned with the Zealots.' The General was obviously surprised at the revelation. 'How can there ever be peace if you keep killing everyone you do not agree with? You do not want peace. You want utter control.'

The King turned on his heel and made his way back to his mount.

Jehu did the same but instead of taking the reins and mounting, he drew a short bow from the side of his horse.

'Look out!' The Captain of the guard shouted as Jehoram vaulted into the saddle and began to gallop from the field.

The arrow struck him in the chest and he toppled from the horse, landing heavily. The wind was knocked from his lungs but as he saw his Captain start to ride to his aid, he put his hand up, palm facing outward.

The Captain slowed his mount as the King yelled his orders. 'My mother. Return….to…. my mother.' The Captain turned his horse and rode from the field as Jehu trotted up to the King.

'We will see if the Lord is with me now, you heathen sod.'

'You may have killed me.' Jehoram took a deep shuddering breath. 'But,' his breathing grew more laboured as blood dripped from the corners of his mouth, 'do not hide behind Yahweh. You seek power, not peace.'

****

Ahaziah saw the dust cloud before he heard fast moving mounted men. He left his grandmother in the tower and took the stairs two at time to the courtyard below.

'Ahaziah, be careful.' Jezebel called after him. She took her seat by the window and watched her grandson mount his horse and canter from the courtyard, his private guard scrambling to follow.

The Captain of the guard led a small troupe of men toward the fortress and slowed when they saw Ahaziah approaching.

'To the fortress your Grace; we must protect the Queen-Mother.'

'Jehoram, where is Jehoram?'

'Jehu has killed him your Grace. An arrow in his back, like the coward he is. He ordered me back to his mother with his last breath.'

'You go to the fortress, protect my grandmother. I will hold them here if I can.' Ahaziah looked around at the near hundred men he had brought with him, all highly trained and seasoned fighting men. He prayed it was enough.

The terrain was wide and Ahaziah knew holding here was going to be too difficult. Jehu's men would only ride around and flank them.

'Follow me!' The King bellowed over the sound of the Captain's retreating horses.

He galloped back toward the fortress. It sat high on a hill, with only one main entrance through the marshalling courtyard. Riding uphill would be difficult for Jehu's men, giving Ahaziah the advantage of higher ground.

He gave the orders and his men split into three groups. Archers sat their mounts, drawing their bows at the ready. The row behind them were mounted swordsmen, who drew their weapons and waited, their horses prancing excitedly. The final rank he sent further up the hill and gave the order to attack any breaches in their defences.

All eyes were on Jehu's men as they slowly cantered their horses forward. They remained out of range for the bowmen and lined up to assess the fortress.

Ahaziah looked over his shoulder to see his grandmother sitting defiantly in the window. His resolve was buffered as she saluted him and smiled.

When the charge came, it was at a full gallop. 'Wait for my order.' Ahaziah warned his bowmen as one arrow loosed before the order. The bowman hastily notched another as the King glared at him.

The sound of horses thundered in Ahaziah's chest, but he took another deep breath before calling his bowmen to release their first round.

Less than ten men went down and the King ordered his men to reload their weapons. 'Prepare!'

This would be their last volley before Jehu's men were too close to use the bows.

'Release!' The King drew his sword and the bowmen followed him.

The second volley struck a few more than the last, but still a formidable force was advancing. 'Where on earth did he find so many sympathisers?' The King asked no-one, for no-one could hear him over the roar that filled his ears.

Ahaziah's mount leapt forward with uncontained adrenalin, while the King raised his sword. He blocked an overhead swing, twisting his sword over the wielder's arm and struck the man in the throat. The soldier went down, taking his mount with him.

The clash of iron on iron rang out as the outnumbered guard did everything to protect their King and his grandmother.

The cavalry surged forward more than once to fill the gap as the fortress guards peppered Jehu's men with arrows from the battlements.

Just as Ahaziah was beginning to believe they could hold this host back, he took a sword to his right shoulder. His sword-arm lost all strength and he dropped his weapon to the ground. Drawing his dagger in his left hand, he fended off another blow before falling from his mount.

On foot now, he ran back toward the fortress, trying to find another horse, sword or even a hatchet, but his vision was growing blurred. He could feel a cold sweat breaking out on his forehead as his vision swam. He opened his eyes to feel coarse gravel on his cheeks, but the absence of sound was what was truly disconcerting. The silence was broken with the soft chuckle of a man he had never met. 'You surprised me Ahaziah. I had not expected such a strong defence from you.'

'Forgive my ignorance. Who are you?'

'I am hurt. Surely you know me, if not by sight, by reputation perhaps.'

'Nothing comes to mind.' Ahaziah knew who he spoke to. Only Jehu would be so bold, so arrogant. 'I am a little tired though, you will understand.'

The man knelt next to Ahaziah and patted him almost affectionately. 'You are dying boy.'

Ahaziah nodded. 'I had guessed as much. You can spare my grandmother. She is unarmed.'

'You grandmother colludes with witch's boy. She is not worthy to rule. Your family never was.'

'And you think you can do better? Good luck with that.'

Jehu frowned as the boy passed out once more. For a moment, he felt like saving him but the line had to die. Each and every member of the family of Ahab would perish if it was the last thing he did.

Instead, Jehu turned and left the King to bleed out on the gravel, focussing his energy on the harlot who had outstayed her welcome in the leadership of Israel.

****

The Captain stood before the Queen-Mother's room. The halls were full of his men when Jezebel opened the door. She had just watched her grandson's life fade before her eyes. She could not bear the thought of more good men dying to save her old bones.

'Stand down Captain. Take your men and hand-in your weapons. The battle is lost.'

'I gave my word your Grace.'

'And I have given you an order. The King is dead. His nephew is dead. I am, for now, your Regent.'

The Captain looked at the greying hair and dark brown eyes of the former Queen and saw the resolve within. He had served the royal family all his life and he would be damned if he was about to shirk his duty this day.

'I have another order for you.' Jezebel seemed to read his thoughts. 'As soon as Jehu gives you leave, you will ride to Jerusalem and warn my daughter.'

The Captain nodded his understanding. He sheathed his sword and bowed before saluting the Queen-Mother and leaving the long, wide hallway.

Jezebel closed the heavy door behind the Captain and returned to her window-seat in time to see Jehu take the stairs to the battlements.

She watched as the Captain spoke briefly with the General and took what was left of his men to the courtyard below. She watched him leave, casting a final look at her in the tower before cantering away.

She had heard Jehu enter her room, but did not turn to look at him. Instead she continued to survey the scene below. Her grandson's body still lay lifeless on the courtyard below. The soldiers milled around as though they had just finished a training exercise and Jezebel's heart sank. What hope was there for mankind when they sought out pain and felt nothing?

'You have no idea how long I have waited for this moment.' Jehu's voice sounded hollow and Jezebel remained facing the window, ignoring the General.

'Your witchcraft, your blasphemy has seen our enemies grow stronger.'

Jezebel had heard enough. 'You are an idiot Jehu. Our enemies grow stronger, not because of my belief or who I worship, but because of your lack of faith. It is too easy to blame someone else for your own inadequacies.'

'I am a fine General. I will be a great King.' Jehu snarled at the older woman who still looked out over the courtyard below, contemptuously.

'Your reign will be shorter than Zimri's. You are a fool to believe killing my family will suddenly give you victory over your enemies.'

'We will see.' Jehu turned to the two servants who had remained with Jezebel. They were both beautifully dressed men with blue eye paint and soft silk robes.

'You, eunuchs.' Both men looked at the General but did not respond, instead they looked to their mistress for instruction. She nodded at them to answer and they both spoke in unison.

'Yes Sir.'

'It is time for our Queen-Mother to die. You will throw her from that window she loves so much.'

Neither man moved. 'You heard me. Do it or die.'

Jezebel could not climb out the window on her own. As much as she longed to do the deed for Jehu and take his power away, she could not throw herself out the window. Instead, she turned to her eunuchs and held out her hands, one for each.

'If you please.' Both men frowned. She returned their concern with a smile. 'It is as it should be. Please. I cannot reach on my own.'

Jehu growled at Jezebel's request. He drew his sword, hoping to finish her before she could martyr herself, but both eunuchs stood in his path, opting to help their mistress.

Jezebel stood on the window sill and could see the Captain's dust cloud in the distance. At least her daughter would have some warning. She jumped into nothingness, a sense of peace washing over her the moment her feet left the sill.

****

Asherah felt her soul would explode, but there was nothing to be done to save Jezebel. Her time was done and her choice had been made. She watched as Jehu's men kicked and trampled the Queen-Mother's body but she had seen to it that Jezebel's soul departed unencumbered. Her body was just that, a remnant of the shell she wore in this earthly realm.

As all Yahweh's children would, Jezebel would find peace. Her soul would be judged by the Redeemer, not by mankind. She would be assessed not on her belief, her intellect, her achievements or her status. She would be judged by her heart and soul and Asherah knew both were worthy.

A broken child of a broken world, she would know peace, when the world knew peace.

For now, Asherah had to ensure the Redeemer came to pass. The bringer of Peace would reign, only if his line survived. She watched Jehu's men ride for Samaria, knowing that when they got there, every child of the Ahab line would be killed to secure the throne of Israel for Jehu.

This was not Yahweh's way. This was the corruption of Elisha the prophet. This was death, and her Father never wanted death. Right from the beginning, He had created life, light, water, warmth, humanity. Why did the people always choose to believe Yahweh wanted death?

Asherah opened her wings and took flight through the veil of space and time. She needed the peace of her home now more than she had ever needed it.

Chapter 26

Sheba watched the service in the temple with disinterest. She had never been concerned with such formal proceedings but since marrying Jehoiada, he had insisted that she learn more about what was involved.

This puzzled the Princess. All the other women were rarely allowed inside the temple courtyard, her wedding being the most recent exception. Usually, they were left outside the courtyard gates to pray while the men knelt on soft mats within the inner courtyard. Only priests and invited guests were allowed inside the holy temple's inner chamber.

They had discussed this at length, but all Jehoiada would say was that she was an exception, being married to a Priest. The Princess did not argue. Women being offered any sort of authority in the temple was rare and Aron had suggested she take what she could get and that it might come in handy later.

Their marriage to date had been amicable. Jehoiada was often tied up with official business and she had been free to spend time with her nephew and Aron. They had shared the marital bed only twice including the wedding night and for some reason, her husband had no objections to her returning to her own apartments within the palace when she was not lying with him.

'Now that is done. Shall we go for a walk?' Jehoiada offered his wife his arm which she accepted with a genuine smile. They walked from the temple, where Aron waited. The Priest nodded acknowledgement to the Princess's body guard who stepped in behind the couple as they left the outer temple courtyard.

They had barely taken a step when a commotion ensued in the wide promenade that separated the temple from the palace. A small group of soldiers in the King's guard uniform rode at speed into the palace courtyard.

'They were Jehoram's men.' Aron spoke as Sheba looked to him for confirmation. 'They look very harassed.'

'Very!' Sheba looked at her husband as she spoke. He had gone a pale shade of grey. 'Are you feeling ill?' She patted his hand as she spoke.

He quickly collected his thoughts. 'No, I am fine my dear. We should see what is happening.'

'Yes, Aron, please lead us to the palace.'

Aron moved forward, his sword-hand hovered cautiously over his hilt. 'Stay behind me Princess. We cannot be sure what this unexpected arrival means.'

They walked quickly along the avenue lined with palm trees and statues of lions. The large sandstone flagstones made the walking easier, but still, the promenade was long and by the time they reached the palace entrance, the horses had been put into the stables and the soldiers had dispersed.

A guard met Aron at the steps to the palace, barring his way. 'The Queen-Mother has given the order that no-one shall enter.'

'Thaliah?' Aron questioned the guard, but he did not remove the spear that crossed the archway beyond.

'You know who I am. This is my home. I will enter.' The Princess reached the top of the stairs having overheard the exchange.

'I am sorry your Grace.' The man bowed, genuinely apologizing for the inconvenience.

Sheba opened her mouth to protest but Aron shook his head so slightly, his eyes warning her not to. 'Princess. Let us break your fast. I am sure your husband is famished.'

'Yes. Of course.' She agreed.

As they moved away, through the courtyard and out of sight, Aron stopped them. 'You should return to the temple Sheba.'

If the familiarity between the two surprised Jehoiada, he did not show it. 'That is very wise my dear.' The Priest had a fairly good idea what was likely to be afoot and he had no desire to get caught up in it.

'You go Jehoiada. I need to see what is going on and check on Joash.'

The Priest turned pale again remembering his oath to Ahaziah. 'Yes, quite right. I should go with you.'

'No.' Aron touched the man's shoulder, eventhough he was quite tall, the Priest seemed to shrink at the touch. 'The Princess knows a few alternative ways into the palace. We will return soon, after we find out what is going on.'

'Very well.' Jehoiada turned and left his wife with her bodyguard, without a backward glance.

'That was too easy.' Sheba remarked as they moved further into the servant quarters of the palace.

'Exactly. I think your husband might know what is happening.'

'I hate the idea, but I believe you could be right.'

They both inhaled the smell of baking bread and smiled as Aron's stomach growled.

'Do you think the cook can spare a little bread on our way through?'

Sheba giggled as Aron's stomach spoke again.

****

'No! You must be mistaken.' Thaliah glared at the Captain of the guard. His face still showed spots of blood which he had not bothered to stop and remove.

'Your mother's last order to me was to get word to you, your Grace.'

'You left Ahaziah to die?'

'No your Grace. Ahaziah died valiantly trying to defend his grandmother.'

'I do not give a fig what he died doing. I told him to save himself.'

The guard looked at the Queen-Mother's personal guards. They did not flinch and he refrained from showing his own reaction.

'I am sorry your Grace. Were you expecting an attack?' The question was delivered without malice, but Thaliah's eyes grew wild.

'Your insolence will not be tolerated.' She took a deep breath preparing to give an order the Captain was sure he did not want to hear.

'I beg your pardon your Grace. I meant no disrespect. I was just unaware anyone but King Jehoram knew his life was under threat.'

'There were rumours. Nothing more.' The Queen-Mother stood and paced upon the dais. The large throne cast shadows over the room and Thaliah touched the arm gently, trying to calm herself.

Ahaziah was supposed to have secured her brother's kingdom, not taken a stand to save him. *He had promised.* This was supposed to be her moment of glory... Ahaziah, King over Israel and her back on the throne of Judah.

The Captain remained silent as he watched the wave of expressions change on the Queen-Mother's face. The final set of her features sent a chill down his spine.

'Leave me now.' The guard bowed respectfully and turned on his heel, leaving the darkened throne room, with its high windows and moody décor behind him.

'Get me a carriage. I need to visit the temple.' The guard on her right bowed and left her side. 'And you. Lock down this palace. No-one enters and no-one leaves unless I give the order.' The guard frowned slightly. 'Do you understand!'.

'Yes your Grace.'

'Yes your Highness.'

'Yes.' The guard bowed more deeply. 'Your Highness.'

 **Chapter 27**

'What is going on? There are guards everywhere!' Aron whispered as he pushed the Princess into a darkened alcove of the hallway and held her behind him. Six guards trotted by in formation, their eyes forward, their focus on something well ahead. Aron sighed in relief.

'We need to find someone who can explain what is going on!' Sheba peered over his shoulder as she whispered in his ear.

They had passed through the cookhouse to gain access to the King's wing. The cooking staff had no idea what was going on. The cook had only shrugged as the Princess asked him a barrage of questions. Finally, Aron decided he needed to snatch some bread and cheese to quiet his stomach and now the couple was unsure of what to do next.

Just as they were about to step from their hidden niche in the wall, they heard more guards. Aron pushed the Princess back into the alcove and she landed heavily against the wall, as two guards left the hallway that led only to the throne room.

'Which temple is she going to?' One guard asked the other as they both exited the passageway leading into the atrium.

'My bet is on Baal.'

'No way!'

'You up for the bet?' The one guard grinned at his friend, who was now rummaging through his coin purse for a copper. He threw it to the guard who laughed. 'Not feeling too confident I see.'

'She is already proving a little unstable. Nothing is a sure bet at the moment. Did you hear what she said?' Both guards were now moving in opposite directions, one to the stables, the other to the main hall.

'Which part, the part about our King taking the throne from her brother, or the part where she was angry that he fought by his side?'

'Both I guess. Time to lock this place down.' The two guards finally parted, leaving Aron and Sheba in the servant's hallway, opened mouthed.

'Is Ahaziah alive?' Sheba held back a sob.

'We should not speculate. At least we have some idea of what is going on.' They were two steps further down the corridor when the Queen-Mother moved from the throne room, lifting her long skirt to avoid tripping over it. Aron pushed the Princess back once more as she rolled her eyes at his back in frustration.

They waited as the Queen rushed through the atrium without a sideways glance, on her way to the palace main entrance.

'I have no intention of staying here if *she* is in charge.'

'I am not sure you get to choose Princess.'

'Does this have anything to do with Jezebel's vision?'

'I would say so. What next?' Aron looked over his shoulder.

'We should go to my apartment so I can gather a few things, then I need to check on Joash.'

Aron nodded and led the way through the King's wing to the royal gardens. From there the pathways would lead them all around the palace, they just needed to avoid the guards or they would be trapped inside the palace.

'Where will Thaliah put everyone if she plans on locking down the palace?'

'The servants will likely be free to roam, but the royal family and Ahaziah's harem will be confined to the women's quarters.'

'So that is where most of the guards will be. We will need to avoid those areas for now.'

'The only way to my apartment is past the women's quarters remember, but I know a few passageways the guards are unlikely to use.'

'You lead the way then.' Aron moved aside and followed Sheba.

As they drew closer to the women's apartments, they could see a group of guards waiting outside. The couple moved from the pathway. Sheba led Aron around the side of a stone wall that was covered in vines, with scattered brightly coloured flowers woven in between.

'Looks like the guards are staying outside for now.' Aron whispered. Sheba nodded and carried on. At the end of the wall she stopped at a well weathered, unpainted wooden door.

As she pulled it open, the smell of mould and mildew wafted out. She almost sneezed, but managed to pinch her nose and resist the sensation.

Aron placed his hand on her back as she ducked into the small entrance. 'Be careful,' he whispered.

****

'You promised me. We had a deal!' Thaliah stood in full royal attire before the Baal priest, her hands on her hips, her expression hostile.

'I promised you that there would be an attack on your brother. Controlling your son was *your* responsibility.' The Priest had a steely look in his eye and the Queen openly scowled at him.

'Jehu will be securing Israel now. I am sure he is massacring Jehoram's entire family as we speak.'

Mattan smiled. He closed his eyes and opened his arms skyward. Thaliah took a step back, puzzled at the Priest's unusual behaviour.

His eyes rolled in his head, showing the white that jostled around like he was having some sort of fit. The strange words that left his lips sounded like they were coming from all directions.

Thaliah's hair blew into the air as though she was in a sandstorm. The room darkened and the Priest's eyes began to shine like balls of fire. The Queen-Mother took another step back from the Priest as her hands began to shake.

'You wanted power Thaliah. You have Judah. You have what you wanted. Now take it!'

Thaliah's heart was beating erratically in her chest. She felt like it was going to force its way out from behind her ribs. She could barely stand, her legs unwilling to obey her commands.

The Priest's body convulsed and he collapsed on the ground. The room became light once more and when Mattan opened his eyes, he seemed disoriented.

'What was all that?' Thaliah asked, her resolve slowly returning.

'What was what?' The Priest forced himself onto shaking legs, reaching for the altar to aid his balance.

'Do not play games with me Mattan.'

'I would never do such a thing. One moment I was listening to you talking of promises I know nothing about, the next, I was waking up on the floor. You tell me what that was all about!'

The Priest looked genuinely horrified and Thaliah looked around the temple with fresh eyes. *Was Baal truly giving her the chance at the power she so desperately desired?*

'Forget about it Mattan. I have already forgotten the incident. I will have need of your services again soon. Make sure you make yourself available.'

The Queen-Mother turned dramatically and moved to the exit. The Priest frowned at her back, wondering once more, what he had done.

****

'Were the theatrics really necessary Baal?' Moloch crossed his arms as Baal joined him once more. They floated above the temple, watching as the Queen-Mother strode from the building.

She took the hand offered by a guard's and stepped up into her carriage. Thaliah looked over her shoulder, then up at the sky as if hoping to see something.

'She needed to know the Priest was not me; that I truly can offer her the power she desires.' Baal looked to his brother, a sense of triumph evident in his eyes.

'Do not let the moment go to your head brother. There is still much to do.'

'Yes, but she will do it now. Of that I am sure. Did you see the look in her eye once she realised I had inhabited the Priest's body? She quivered with excitement.'

'She quivered, but I am not entirely sure it was excitement.'

'I think she understands the *deal* she has made. I do not believe my tone left any misunderstanding.'

'Come, let us keep an eye on the proceedings.' Moloch moved from the temple, taking flight with his huge wings.

Baal followed. 'Jerusalem is plagued by death. It is almost a curse you know.'

Moloch laughed. 'It is plagued by you brother, not a curse.'

Baal joined in on the jest as Thaliah's carriage drew up in front of the palace and she began barking orders to whoever was within earshot.

Chapter 28

Isaac watched from his hiding place on the battlements. As far as guards went, Jerusalem's were certainly not the most astute.

There were men running everywhere in disarray, but with a purpose that Isaac struggled to decipher. The only word he had received from Jehu was the note he now held in his hand.

He had read it over, and over again. Now as he opened it, and read it again, he shook his head.

The dove will fall.

He had seen the dove enter the palace with Aron, through the cookhouse. He knew then that something was amiss. That was shortly followed by the Queen-Mother screaming at her carriage driver to go faster.

Now she was back, barking orders as men ran like scared rats around the courtyard. Weapons were being pulled from the armoury and servants were being herded like sheep into groups.

He climbed down the stone wall, one foot-hold and hand-hold at a time, until he reached the rear of the cookhouse. He needed to track down his brother, but he was unfamiliar with the palace interior.

As he made to step over a pathway into the cover of the trees, he pulled back, hugging the stone wall, in the shadows, not daring to take another breath.

Four fully armed men ran past at a slow jog, heading toward the centre of the palace.

The assassin jumped over the pathway as they moved away, hunkered down into the foliage and followed the four guards. They were met by another group of ten, all in battle armour and fully armed.

Isaac frowned. Why would armed men be heading into the palace, not manning the walls? An attack would come from outside, not within. Unless?

A sense of urgency the assassin had not had since he was a boy rushed into his veins. He had to find Aron and quickly.

****

Sheba emerged from the tunnel and moved into the courtyard in front of her apartment. The sound of squealing and crying came to her instantly and she turned to see Aron drawing his sword.

'Get to your room,' he ordered and the Princess rushed to her veranda.

'I need my sword.' Sheba stepped inside, Aron followed, holding the door slightly ajar, watching for any trouble while she pulled open a chest that sat at the foot of her bed.

'Soldiers.' Aron spoke softly and pushed the door closed, holding the handle so the latch would not make any noise.

'In the courtyard?' Sheba questioned, as she removed her sword and closed the lid on the chest

Aron only nodded, moving to the window. He discreetly pulled the curtain back just a sliver. The guards moved past Sheba's room. She was not supposed to be here. There was no reason for them to come and check.

He turned to find the Princess naked as she pulled on her training tunic and tied her sword belt in place. The weapon knocked a candlestick on her nightstand and Aron gasped as it teetered precariously before the Princess snatched it in her hand.

She released a quiet, nervous giggle before placing it on her bed for safe keeping.

'Where to now?' Aron asked, still watching out the window.

'Joash. No matter what this is all about, he is my priority right now.'

'Agreed.' Aron stepped away from the window and took the Princess in his arms, placing a firm kiss on her lips. She reached up and grasped the back of his head, holding him to her until she had no breath remaining.

Aron moved to the door, turned the knob completely and pulled the door open a crack. He listened a moment before opening it wide and ushering Sheba through.

The Princess moved cautiously back to the hidden passage they had just left and ducked inside. She heard guards rushing in her direction and waited for Aron to join her. When he did not, she put her hand to her lips to stop herself from calling out to him.

She closed her eyes and listened. There was no clash of swords, no shouting, so where was he? She jumped as he joined her. He could not see her face in the darkened tunnel, but he felt the punch that landed on his bicep.

'What took you so long?'

'I am fine Princess. Thanks for caring.' Aron whispered back, the smile not seen on his face, was evident in his voice.

Even in the stone tunnel, more screams, more cries reached them as they neared the women's apartments. Sheba shivered as the sound grew louder. She opened the old rickety door to the gardens beyond and moved into the daylight.

The colour drained from her face when she realised what she was hearing. Women were screaming, begging for their lives, the lives of their children. The sounds of crying were being replaced with screams of agony.

Aron moved to the crenel that allowed air to move around the women's courtyard. The small pool for swimming stood surrounded by low rows of jasmine. As Sheba moved to look through, Aron stopped her with his palm on her chest. He shook his head, but she pushed him aside.

The fountain that ran into the pool ran red. She saw a soldier wipe his blade on the dress of one of her brother's consorts, the body unrecognisable. Inside the building, women were still screaming, the sounds of grunting men leaving nothing to the imagination.

'These are our own guards.' Sheba could barely speak.

'I know.' Aron pulled her away from the courtyard wall.

'We have to save them,' she begged, but Aron shook his head.

'Joash. We only have time to find Joash. Where are the children?'

The idea of their own men, killing the women and children brought out a cold sweat on Sheba's hands. She wiped them on her tunic and tried to focus.

The sound of moving shrubs behind them caused them both to bring their swords to bear.

'What the hell are you doing here? Stop dawdling and get the girl out.' Isaac pointed his sword at the Princess, while not taking his eyes from Aron.

'What are you doing here?' Aron challenged.

'No time to discuss.' Isaac moved off toward the palace entrance.

'I have no idea who you are, but we are not leaving my nephew here.'

Isaac turned to Aron and smiled. 'I can see why you like her brother. Suit yourself. It is your funeral.'

'Are you going to help us?' Aron asked, suddenly feeling apprehensive. He looked to Sheba for confirmation, realising she now knew who he was.

'Not likely.' Isaac turned to leave.

'Then why did you come? Was it to kill me? Well here is your chance.' Sheba challenged.

'Yes, originally, but now…'

Aron used Isaac's indecision. 'Join me brother. Help me find Joash and we can all leave, together.'

'I was getting bored.' Isaac smiled and nodded in the direction the couple had been heading. 'After you.'

Chapter 29

Jehoiada could not stop shaking. The sound of death floated on the wind toward the temple and as much as he was afraid of losing Sheba, he could not bring himself to go and find her.

'She is with Aron.' He reassured himself aloud. 'He will not let anything happen to her.'

The Priest knew his wife's bodyguard loved her as much as he did. He even had his suspicions about how close they were, but it was easier to push them to the back of his mind.

The sun had begun to set on the turmoil that was going on within the walls of the palace. Jehoiada wrapped his robe around his neck and decided he had only one course of action left to him.

He lit the candles on the seven-armed golden Menorah and knelt before the altar. Closing his eyes, he began his prayer. The sound of his melodic voice filled the chamber and with every word that left his lips, he felt the very walls sigh in emotional relief.

Asherah heard the melody of the prayer echo through the veil. She flew to the temple, hovering over it to watch. Her heart ached for the man. She could not comfort him, for in his eyes, she was a heathen god, something to be repulsed.

The sound of people dying filled her senses and she looked to the palace, realising it was under attack. She flew at full speed to investigate, but as she neared, she was struck by an unseen barrier that knocked the energy from her body. As she slid to the world below, she was caught by something.

Moloch cradled the Goddess in his arms and gently placed her on her feet, atop a nearby roof.

'What is happening?' Asherah looked around, trying to get her bearings. 'The barrier is yours?'

'It is.'

'Then why catch me? Why not let me plummet to the ground?'

'Because the barrier is not meant to hurt you sister.'

'What is it meant to do?'

'Shield you from the pain.' Moloch looked into Asherah's eyes with genuine regret. The sound of laughter, Baal's laughter filled the air, unheard by anyone around them.

'Shut up brother.' Moloch reprimanded Baal who looked questioningly at his mentor.

'Why? The women and children are dying. Is that not what you wanted?'

'I take no pleasure in this Baal. This is necessary.'

'No! It is not *necessary*.' Asherah flew into the air, attempting once more to breach the barrier. 'How did you keep me out?'

'If not for that mournful Priest, you would not have known until it was over.' Moloch spoke almost apologetically.

'Known what?' Anath and Astarte spoke in unison as they too heard the Priest's prayers.

'Moloch has created a barrier to shield us from interfering in his plans.' Asherah pointed to the palace below. There were bodies all over the courtyard. Even the servants had been executed.

'Oh Father. Look at all those bodies. Who is attacking them?' Anath flew toward the barrier.

'No! Anath. You cannot get through.' The Goddess halted, her wings extended as she hovered above the unseen barrier.

'What is going on?' Astarte flew toward Anath, peering down on the dying people below.

'Yes Moloch! What is going on?' Asherah flew close to Moloch, tapping his chest with her pointer finger.

'Thaliah is killing all of Ahaziah's heirs.'

'Oh brother. The Line!'

'The very same.' Moloch felt the weight of his actions now, but the decision had been made.

'Why?' Astarte drew her sword and moved forward, but Anath moved between her and Moloch.

'No Astarte. This is *not* what Father would want.'

'I am sick of guessing what Father would want.' Astarte pushed Anath aside and growled at Moloch.

'This is accomplishing nothing sister.' Asherah placed a barrier between her brethren. 'We need to focus on saving all those innocent lives.'

'We are not supposed to meddle.' Anath offered unconvincingly.

'Moloch has already done just that.'

'I did not make the woman kill her grandchildren.'

'No, as is your custom you simply manipulate and step back to watch.' Asherah dropped the barrier as Astarte lowered her sword.

'Contrary to popular myth, I am not an eater of babies.'

'You do nothing to stop the myth though brother.' Baal smiled at the ongoing scene before him. 'This really is amusing. I must have you over more often.' He addressed the entire group. 'It is such a lovely catch up with family.'

'Drop the barrier Moloch. What is done now cannot be undone, but if what you say is true and you really do not relish the death of these children, then lift the barrier and let us help.'

Moloch shook his head. 'The Redeemer's line must end sister or we will remain in servitude to them for eternity.'

Asherah knew there was no stopping Moloch without a fight and Gabriel had been clear on that matter.

'Come sisters,' she spoke to Anath, who grabbed Astarte by the arm and dragged her away.

'Where are they going?' Baal watched as the three angels opened their wings and launched into the air.

'Off to find Gabriel or Michael I would expect. We have little time left before we will be forced to drop the barrier. Let us hope it is long enough.'

****

Thaliah covered her ears. Even in the depths of the throne room, the sounds drifted through the high windows that allowed such little light to filter in.

Her vision swam with memories of Ahaziah as a newborn in her arms; his tiny hands and feet with each perfect digit in its place, touching her naked body as she fed him for the first time.

Now he was gone, just like that. All her plans to rule over all of Israel were falling from her grasp. Now Jehu would rule in Israel and it was only a matter of time before he moved against her in Judah.

Killing the heirs was the only way to stop Jehu from launching an immediate attack. Jehu would see her as too weak to be a threat. With no heir to take the throne, her time was limited to her own lifespan.

Jehu was young enough; he had time to wait before launching an assassination. Thaliah wondered how best to use that time. The sounds grew too loud to endure. She reached into her robe and pulled out the last vial, removing the stopper, before swallowing the fluid in one mouthful.

As the liquid entered her body, she felt the weightlessness wash over her. The sounds of crying babies and screaming mothers blurred into nothing as the room began to float like clouds on a sunny day.

Chapter 30

There was little resistance offered to the palace guards as they swept through the servant's quarters and the royal family apartments. The soldiers helped themselves to the King's wine stores and began drinking as they lounged around the courtyards and royal gardens.

'The nursery is through there.' Sheba pointed to a pathway that led straight past a group of at least ten soldiers.

Aron raised his head above the hedge of primrose and followed the Princess's line of sight. 'Is there a back entrance? A tunnel?' Aron almost pleaded.

'No.' Sheba spoke softly as Aron joined her once more behind the cover of the hedge.

'A frontal attack it is then,' Isaac proposed.

'They are drunk,' Aron offered. 'Try to kill as many soundlessly as we can.' Isaac rolled his eyes at his brother who suddenly understood the irony of the statement.

'We will have very little time if the sound of iron on iron rings out. This entire massacre has been without any altercation,' the

Princess offered. 'I think a distraction is in order. Let us see if Thaliah has given the order to kill me, along with my family.'

Aron grabbed her by the arm, but Isaac stopped him. 'She makes a valid point brother. Either way, she will know if she too is a target or not.'

'They may not know one royal from another. Be careful Sheba.'

As the Princess moved away on hands and knees, Isaac looked at his brother's expression. 'She will be fine. When did you realise you were in love with her?'

'When I trained her.'

'When was that?' Isaac peered over the hedge to assess the soldiers and his surroundings as he spoke.

'I left when she was in her fifteenth year. Her father realised we were growing close. Were you really sent to kill her?'

Isaac drew the note from his pocket and handed it to Aron. *The Dove will fall.*

'Jehu?' Isaac merely nodded as Aron whispered his assumption.

'Thank you,' Aron mouthed as he heard Sheba's voice from behind the bushes.

'We had best move. I can see at least two soldiers who can be dispatched without a distraction.' Isaac nodded to two younger men who had fallen unconscious from excessive wine. They were both leaning against a stone wall that was out of sight from the main group.

Aron moved first, with Isaac right behind him. They both drew daggers from their thigh scabbard as they moved.

The younger of the two looked like he was barely old enough to shave. Aron shook his head as Isaac loomed over the second man.

'What on earth are you men doing?' Sheba's voice startled the two young soldiers whose eyes popped open as their mouths were covered and a blade sliced across their throats.

Aron and Isaac held their mouths and sat on their legs to prevent them from thrashing as the lifeblood drained from them.

'You are fairly good at this. Maybe you should have joined me in my profession,' Isaac whispered with a wicked grin.

The men before Sheba had jumped to a wavering attention at the authoritative tone the Princess used. They were trying desperately to focus through bleary eyes.

'I asked you a question. Surely the Queen asked you to report back after you completed your work, not dally around here like common thugs?'

Two older soldiers who could hold their liquor far more successfully than the others looked at each other. The confusion was quickly replaced with recognition.

Sheba remained calm on the outside, but inside her mind was screaming at her to run. The soldier on the right was a heavy-set man with an angry red scar running down his left cheek. His eyes tunnelled into the Princess, who reflexively tensed her sword-arm.

It was all the warning he needed. He drew his weapon, while the other soldier, still uncertain, joined him, looking apprehensively from the Princess to his friend.

'Your name was not exactly discussed Princess. The Queen was fairly general in her order.'

'Discussed where? Put away your weapons you imbeciles. It is the Queen who sent me to check up on the progress.'

Sheba had not drawn her weapon in response. The soldier hesitated. 'The children are all dead,' he answered, deciding on caution. He could have misunderstood the Queen. The Priest's wife was not supposed to be in the palace.

Sheba failed to keep her anger in check at such a disgusting revelation delivered so casually.

'You killed *all* the children? That was mighty brave of you. How many put up a fight?' The sarcasm confused the man momentarily, just long enough for Aron and Isaac to step up behind two more guards who had been watching with casual interest.

The man with the scar growled as he realised the Princess was not alone.

'What! You thought I would be an easy target?' Sheba pushed her anger aside. She knew it would serve no purpose in this fight.

The man moved forward with his friend trailing close behind. The Princess drew her weapon and the soldier laughed condescendingly.

'What do you plan to do with that?' He nodded to her lighter weight weapon that Aron had commissioned.

The Princess did not answer, instead she let the sword respond. The weapon was more flexible than the heavy swords of the Royal Guard and with its lighter weight, Sheba could move it quickly to where she chose.

The sword struck the soldier in his off-side forearm, but before he could respond, the Princess tossed her weapon to her other hand and swung it around to slice the man's thigh.

He jumped back, suddenly feeling less confident. 'Maakha. Get your butt out here! Where is Sahar, you useless twits,' the man called as the soldier behind him moved forward to face the Princess.

'Oh, you mean the two child soldiers? It saddens me to say we had to put them to sleep.' Isaac grinned in a way that sent chills down the man's spine.

'Take her Kaleb.' The soldier instructed the man now facing the Princess.

Aron stepped forward as two men rushed at him. 'Quietly.' He warned Isaac as he side-stepped the first soldier's wild, slightly drunken swing, striking him at the base of his skull on the way by.

The man slumped to the ground like a sack of flour, while his companion faltered. Aron pierced his chest, causing air and blood to bubble from his mouth as he sank to the ground.

Isaac had been true to his word. Both his opponents were dead without so much as a mutter. Aron nodded his approval. 'They were hardly a challenge with a belly full of wine.' Isaac opened his hands, palm up and shrugged.

Sheba was moving back from her attacker, trying to avoid sword contact. Every step he took, she dodged. Every swing, she ducked under or around.

Aron moved toward the Princess as the man with the scar suddenly felt his courage returning. He launched himself at Aron, only to meet his end, a dagger protruding from his back.

Aron threw his own blade as Sheba was running out of room to manoeuvre. She tripped over the low hedge and landed heavily on her backside, as the blade sailed past her left ear, striking the man in his right eye. He fell to the ground on top of the Princess, who struggled under his weight.

Aron and Isaac reached Sheba at the same time, pulling the dead man clear. The Princess, still on her backside on the grass, screwed up her nose in disgust. 'I would have had him, if I could have used this sword property,' she offered defensively.

'I have no doubt.' Isaac reached out and she took his hand, while Aron scanned the courtyard.

'Where did the other two go?'

'There were ten guards. We only killed eight.' Aron searched the surrounding area with Isaac.

'Ah, these two.' Isaac kicked one who remained unconscious, a wineskin spilling red wine onto his chest.

'We need to check the children.' Sheba moved toward the apartment.

'Why? The guards said they are were all dead.' Isaac was genuinely perplexed.

'Are you serious? I need to make sure Joash was not amongst them.'

'Why would he not be?' Aron followed the Princess, catching her by the arm and pulling her into an embrace.

'I do not know, but I need to check. I just do.' Aron nodded as the Princess wrenched herself from his grasp and launched into a run, entering the children's play area with a sudden stop.

'Oh my God!' The room was covered in blood. 'She ran to the nearest child who was the same age as Joash and knelt beside the unrecognisable body. Only the clothing gave her any hint that this was one of Ahaziah's daughters, not his son.

'We should go.' Aron knelt next to Sheba who held back tears with every ounce of strength she could draw on.

Isaac stood by the doorway, his eyes roaming the room, taking in all the destruction. There were so many dead he could not begin to count the bodies.

A young woman, likely a nursemaid lay on top of the bodies of three, possibly four small children. She had shielded them with her body, but they were still dead. The soldiers had simply thrust spears and swords through her body until everything stopped moving.

He had seen massacres such as this and he knew only too well what a gruesome death these young souls would have endured.

He was about to leave the room when something caught his eye. 'Aron.' His brother looked at Isaac and frowned.

'I know. We need to go.'

'No. Look!' Isaac pointed to a pile of bodies in the middle of the room. Two nursemaids had done as the first had, thrown their bodies on top of the smaller children, hoping to save them. But just below one of them, the hand of a toddler could be seen. 'I swear I saw that little hand move.'

'Listen.' Aron instructed.

Sheba held her tears back and stopped breathing while all three watched the blood-smeared pile of clothing before them. 'There. Did you hear that?' Aron said as he stood. Sheba did not wait. She rushed past her lover and started pulling bodies from the massacre without even thinking.

'Here, let me.' Isaac moved forward. 'This is not work for a Princess.'

'This is my family. I have seen the birth of every one of these children.' Aron took her bloody hands and held them in his while Isaac dug deeper into the pile, where entrails fell and blood ran.

'Let him Sheba.' Aron hugged her close to his body and wrapped his arms around her as she began to shiver with the shock he knew would come.

'Here.' Isaac pulled a now unconscious baby from the pile and Sheba almost screamed as she saw the curly mop of hair.

'Joash. Oh thanks be to Yahweh.' She cradled the child in her arms and kissed his bloody forehead repeatedly.

'Come, we need to get out of here before someone finds those guards dead or the others wake up.' Isaac started to leave.

'Where are we going to take him?' Aron voiced his thought aloud.

'The temple.' Sheba offered as she stood, still holding Joash's face to her chest.

'You cannot trust the Priest,' Isaac offered. 'He knew about the attack on your brother and uncle.'

The Princess looked at Isaac and considered his words. 'We had our suspicions, but Jehoiada is a High Priest of Yahweh and Joash is the only remaining heir to the line of King David. He will not betray the boy.'

Aron took Joash so that Sheba could move more quickly. He was a toddler, but he was still heavy. 'Sheba is right. If Jehoiada had anything to do with the Zealots, then their plans could have anticipated this.'

'No. This is Thaliah's doing. I swear it must be her way of punishing the Zealots for killing Ahaziah.' The Princess wiped Joash's still features as Aron carried him over his shoulder.

The trio left with the heir and moved past the bodies in the courtyard. They found the tunnel that would take them back to the cookhouse and then hoped that if the revelry continued, they would be able to leave via the servant's quarters unhindered.

Chapter 31

Gabriel and Michael descended upon the city of Jerusalem. Their wings we so huge, that they would have blocked out the fading sunlight if they had not been in their astral form.

Gabriel reached out to feel the barrier removed and turned to Asherah to see her face full of anguish.

'They are gone Asherah. The barrier is down.' He cast his eye upon the massacre below and his face softened. 'Remember what I said to you?' Asherah nodded to the Archangel, who looked at Michael. Both nodded and spread their wings wide as they shot into the heavens like a starburst.

Asherah floated silently over the palace. The bodies of the innocent were everywhere. The grass of the royal garden was splattered with blood, even the flowers were red.

The moon was rising as the final sliver of sunlight faded. The sound of Jehoiada's prayer still drifted to her ears. Her heart ached at the tragic loss. 'I will never forgive you for this Moloch.' She spoke to the air, knowing he would be able to hear her.

'You play with their lives like they mean nothing to you. You say sacrifices must be made for the greater good, your greater good. There is no good while you stand by and allow this to happen brother.'

The air around the Goddess moved and she felt her brother's presence, but he did not show himself.

Instead, she focussed her attention on the trio huddled behind the cookhouse. There were guards everywhere. They had little hope of making it out safely. She sighed, knowing she could not take a life to help them.

****

'You need both hands to fight.' Sheba protested. 'Let me take Joash.'

'No, if they see us with the child, they will tell Thaliah he lives. She will scour the city to find him.' Aron looked around as though an idea was formulating in his mind.

'What are you looking for?' Isaac asked.

'I need something to make a sling from. I can strap the boy to my back. In the low light, they will not know he is anything but a bundle of equipment or spare clothing.'

Isaac nodded. 'I will find something. Wait here.' The assassin dropped to all fours and disappeared into the growing darkness.

'He is good?' Sheba whispered her question.

'He is a professional. If anyone can move around unnoticed, it will be Isaac.'

'How did he become an assassin and you a soldier?'

'We both joined the army together. We were all that was left of our family after our parents died. Isaac was angry that he could not protect them, or that they had left him. I am still not sure.' Aron shifted the still unconscious prince to his lap and Sheba stroked the boy's hair, now matted with dried blood.

'Whenever we trained, he would grow more vicious than most. Our commanding officer realised Isaac had no filter when it came to death.' Aron shrugged. 'His talent was wasted in the regular army. He was taken away and trained as an assassin.'

'Did you see him much during that training?' Joash stirred but did not open his eyes. The Princess kissed his brow again and whispered reassurances into his ear.

'No. I had not seen him again until the other week, when I knew he had to be here to kill someone.'

Sheba lent forward and kissed him on the cheek. 'He is helping us now,' she reassured him.

The moon was full in the sky by the time Isaac returned. The guards were milling around the entrance to the courtyard and there was no simple way of making it past them—not without a fight.

Aron wrapped Joash in a cook's apron, making sure to tuck his arms and his legs into the makeshift hammock. He then took another apron and wrapped it around the entire swaddling, cradling him like a cocooned caterpillar. Isaac tied the boy to the bodyguard's back securely.

Sheba rubbed the boy's back affectionately and nodded that she was ready to move.

Both men shuffled on all fours as they made their way into the garden, sticking to the back of the hedge as they crawled around the courtyard as far as the garden would allow.

Sheba followed them. Her short tunic a blessing for this manoeuvre, but she was fighting not to shiver in the cool night air.

Although there were so many guards, most were inebriated. Their only hope was that Isaac and Aron could fight their way through the few sober guards that blocked their exit, but they both knew their chances were slim.

The brothers looked at each other and drew their swords. Sheba followed their example and the trio stood in unison. They moved silently at first, approaching the large archway that offered them freedom, until one guard saw them, some twenty paces out.

What followed next was nothing short of pandemonium. Nearly every soldier's eyes fell on them as they began to run, full speed toward their escape.

Two guards nearly fell over themselves to the right, trying to get to their feet quickly, yet too drunk to even stand.

Aron and Isaac crossed swords with three guards that stood between them and the opening. Sheba swung to her right, blocking a sword heading straight at Aron's back and the concealed Joash.

The guard's eyes grew wide as he realised the Princess was armed. She used his surprise to her advantage, charging in to his stomach with her shoulder. He grunted and fell to the ground.

The ring of iron on iron brought more guards from all directions. 'We knew it was a long shot.' Isaac offered with a shrug. Aron grinned at his brother without looking at him.

Aron's sword sliced through the shoulder of one of the three men still blocking their way. The guard dropped to his knees, clutching his shoulder as Aron's sword opened his throat.

Another guard found an opening in Isaac's defence as he tried to keep both his opponents at bay. The assassin did not flinch as a deep cut opened on his left cheek.

More soldiers joined the two remaining, preventing the trio's escape. Sheba blocked another blow aimed at their rear. This time, she used her sword to its full extent, taking the attacker in the chest. Her blade lodged there and for a moment, the Princess panicked. More guards were right behind him and she had no weapon.

Aron saw her dilemma. 'Here!' He threw his sword to her, the hilt keeping it weighted down for her to catch it mid-air. He bent under a wild swing, grabbing the man's arm and breaking it. Taking the guard's sword he turned it over in his palm, sending the blade into his attacker's throat.

The sound of the man's gurgling breath was all Sheba could hear as another guard attacked her.

The trio was surrounded, backs pushed together in a small circle, swords raised defensively and nowhere else to go. Sheba silently spoke Asherah's name as a wind began to stir in the courtyard.

The coarse gravel became airborne and the trio covered their eyes to protect themselves. The wind grew so fierce that Sheba thought she might be carried away, but Aron reached for her and the trio turned inward, locking shoulders with one another.

The sound of guards being tossed like weeds could be heard and Sheba risked a glance. The force of the wind was so strong, that the guards were either pushed back, or thrown into the wall by it.

As the wind passed over them, it took guards and debris with it, until only they were left in total stillness. Aron and Isaac exchanged glances, as the wind continued behind them. Guards leant against the force, trying to reach them, but to no avail.

'Time to go,' Isaac instructed as Aron pulled Sheba by the hand, through the archway and down the promenade until they reached the first branch of alleyways.

'We need to…get to the temple…but we cannot… be seen.' Aron offered between deep breaths as he ran. They moved into the darkened alleyway and stopped to quickly regain their breath before moving on.

The moon shone high in the sky as they navigated the many corridors that led them past the marketplace and on into the less desirable areas of the city. A man with a short blade jumped out of the darkness only to see both

Isaac and Aron and decide that running was his best option.

Finally, sure there was no-one pursuing them, the trio made their way to the temple. The courtyard looked eerie in the moonlight, devoid of any life. Sheba led them through the vestibule expecting to find Jehoiada in his adjacent apartment, but he was prostrate on the floor before the altar, the Menorah candles burning low.

'Priest.' Isaac spoke first. Jehoiada was jolted awake by the strange voice but recognised Sheba instantly.

'Oh! Thank Yahweh. I was so afraid for you.'

'Not afraid enough to come find her.' Isaac's tone was acidic.

'It was horrific Jehoiada.' The Princess began untying the bundle from Aron's back, while the Priest frowned at the close contact. 'Thaliah has killed my entire family.'

'Thaliah? I do not understand.'

Aron helped Sheba untie the second layer as the Priest looked on, the question in his eyes not yet leaving his lips.

'We found Joash. He needs food and a physician's care.' The Priest gasped as the layer of fabric revealed a child covered in blood, his body limp and his colour below the red stain, grey and pale.

'Bring him to my rooms, quickly.' An acolyte slept in the corner of the vestibule, undisturbed by unexpected visitors. 'Imar, quickly, boil me some water, find me some goat's milk. Bring it to my rooms. *Move* boy.'

The acolyte rubbed his eyes as he ran from the temple, almost bumping into a huge pillar on the way out.

Aron had said nothing, but now as the Priest cradled the child, he could see he knew nothing of Thaliah's part in this atrocity.

They followed the Priest through the vestibule and the preparation room, on into the Priest's rooms. The Priest turned, looking for a place to put the child. Sheba began pulling back the covers of the Priest's bed. Aron caught an unmistakable look in his eye as he looked at Joash in his arms.

'You knew.' Jehoiada met his eyes and averted his gaze instantly.

'I knew very little.' He moved toward his bed.

Isaac wished now he had kept the note to Jehu but he remained silent. He had no proof.

'You knew what?' Aron pressed.

'I hardly think a *bodyguard*, even one as *close* as you are to the Princess should be questioning *me*.'

Isaac had heard enough. 'We know you were involved with the Zealots and I know the contents of the note you sent to Jehu. Do you wish me to repeat it here?'

Jehoiada went pale and shook his head. He sighed as his shoulders admitted defeat. 'I knew Jehu planned treason. I was not privy to the details, but I expected he was targeting your uncle and brother.'

Sheba did not know if she wanted to cry or hit him. The latter won out as she slapped his face, the sound echoing through the halls.

Their conversation was interrupted as the acolyte returned, a skin of milk in one hand, and a large kettle of hot water in the other.

'We will finish this conversation after Joash is safe.' Sheba took the child away from the Priest, who seemed reluctant to give him up. As she placed him on the bed, she motioned the acolyte over and took the skin from his hand. 'Prepare a bath. I need to feed him first. Then find a physician.'

The men collected up a basin and poured half the hot water into it, while the Princess tried to get the boy to open his mouth to take a drop of milk. He was still unconscious, so she smeared a layer of milk on his lips, but he did not move.

'Here.' Aron reached for the boy. 'Let us warm him up, maybe he will stir enough to feed.' He undressed the child, discarding the sticky red garments into a pile. As he lowered the boy into the basin, his body stirred, but his eyes did not open.

Sheba soaked a cloth and began working at the boy's face. It was impossible to see if the blood were his or not until she finally removed it all.

He was untouched. Not even a graze. His nursemaid had taken every blow of the swords and not one had penetrated the boy, but he was not safe yet. If he did not eat, he would die.

Chapter 32

Thaliah awoke to silence. The screaming had stopped and the entire palace was deadly quiet.

Why had no-one woken her? Where were her servants? Where was her morning meal? She threw her bedspread to the floor and moved toward her window.

She pulled the thick curtain aside and froze as her heart began to race. The entire courtyard was covered in soldiers. They were laid out in awkward positions and none was moving.

She squinted, trying to decide if they were alive or asleep, but finally considered the only way to be sure was to go down and see for herself.

She dressed quickly, draping her most regal robe over her shoulders for dramatic effect. She was the Queen once more and no-one, no-one could do anything about it. She smiled to herself as she opened the door, still expecting to see a guard posted beyond or a servant meandering up the hall ready to serve her meal.

The hallways were deserted. There was not even a maid dusting the stone mantles or balustrading. As she walked down the stairs leading to the courtyard, she saw that some of her soldiers were indeed dead, while most were merely grazed and bloodied, nursing their wounds like little children.

'What is going on here?' She surveyed the group, looking for someone who would take responsibility. A short, heavy-set soldier moved forward and bowed.

'Your Highness.' She smiled at the use of her new title. She never did like the term '*Your Grace*'.

'Report!'

'Your orders were carried out. Every member of your household was' he searched for the right word 'eliminated.'

'Very good. Where are the servants?' The Queen looked around the courtyard, trying to find anyone who might be able to organise her a meal. 'I am famished.'

'Yes your Highness. About that.' The Queen frowned and the man visibly shivered. 'You see the men got a little carried away.'

'And.' The Queen pushed, suddenly realising the gravity of the situation.

'Well, they killed everyone your Highness. Indiscriminately.'

'So, what you are saying is that they cannot follow a simple order? Kill my son's brats and all his harem, not my damned servants! You had better fetch me some more. Now!' The guard made to move but the Queen suddenly realised something.

'Who attacked you? Why are you all bloodied and why are some of your men dead?'

'A group of three escaped. The Princess and her bodyguard, with one other.'

The look on the Queen's face was hard to read and the guard moved back a step instinctively.

'Sheba was here? That was not supposed to happen. Send word to the temple, an offer of my utmost and sincere apologies to my step daughter and her husband, the High Priest. She has safe passage in the palace and I would like to honour her as my guest.'

'Yes, your Gr.. Highness. I will see to it.'

'And clean up this mess.' The Queen swung around and sniffed at the dishevelled bunch of misfits her son had called his palace guard, before remembering, he had taken most of his elite soldiers with him.

****

Aron stood just inside the gates to the temple courtyard and watched the wagons roll out of the palace gates, loaded high with the bodies of the dead. He shook his head at the accompanying line of hopeful peasants, waiting to see if they could gain employment in service to the new Queen.

'How quickly they forget. Or do they just not care?' Aron asked Isaac who stood at the other side of the temple entrance. They were still unsure if they should expect trouble. The guards must have recognised them, but they would not have seen Joash.

'They are hungry and have families to feed. One man's loss, is another man's gain.'

'That is sad.'

'No. It is life brother. You have always been different from most. You set your expectations high, and expect everyone to be capable of your standards. They are not. Most men would have selfishly taken their lover away from her life and kept her to themselves.'

Isaac smiled at Aron's shock. 'How long have you known?'

'Almost from the moment I saw you together. But then I followed you, to the poor quarter.' Aron nodded. There was no need for his brother to explain.

'I just do not understand how people cannot see the bigger picture? Do they not understand that they feed a monster? She will gain power and she will just as easily kill the next group of servants without a second thought.'

'Most people are sheep brother. They are content to follow along, eating, sleeping, rutting and reproducing. You and I, we are different, but we both took very opposite paths. The sheep are harmless. It is you and I who are dangerous.' Isaac cleaned his fingernails with the tip of his dagger as he seemed to have taken his mind elsewhere.

Aron watched as a plume of smoke began to rise on the hillside behind the palace. The bodies of an entire line of the royal family were being incinerated and the world was just carrying on as if nothing were amiss.

He walked across the courtyard toward the temple steps, but as he looked upon the high walls, with the shining marble floor gleaming in the sunlight of a new day he felt only sorrow. He shook his head and sighed. What hope was there for people who only thought of themselves first? It was a dog-eat-dog world to exist in and he felt the weight of it on his shoulders.

Maybe he should have taken Sheba and lived a simple life as a farmer, playing with his children, growing food and feeding his family. He chuckled to himself as he forced his melancholy away.

As he entered the temple, he made his way through the vestibule and into the Priest's quarters to check on Sheba. The sound of laughter greeted him as he descended the stairs and he reached the bottom to see Joash's smiling face over the Princess's shoulder.

'We will raise him, but we must keep him out of sight. If Thaliah discovers he is alive, she will kill us all.' Jehoiada looked up over Sheba's shoulder as Aron came into his view.

'You still have not explained to us your involvement in all of this Priest. I am not sure Sheba is safe here with you.'

'I would never allow any harm to come to Sheba. I made a promise to the King.'

'Yes, the very same King who is now dead because you did not warn him of Jehu's plot.' Aron stood alongside the Princess, trying to keep his tone civil as he ruffled Joash's hair.

'I told you before. I knew no details of what Jehu planned.'

'But you suspected. You still could have warned Ahaziah.' There was silence as Jehoiada stared into Aron's eyes.

'Yes, but our ideals were aligned at the time.'

'Really!' Sheba looked at her husband with shock. 'What ideals? Killing the anointed leaders of our nation?'

'No, not that. The removal of Baal's temples and his priests from our lands.'

'Well that has not exactly worked out very well now has it? Thaliah has been a worshipper of Baal for years and now she is sure to raise the temple to a greater significance than it has experienced in years,' Aron challenged as he took Joash from Sheba's arms. The little boy held out his hands to her bodyguard and giggled as he embraced him.

Jehoiada watched the bodyguard with a sense of jealously, that he struggled to hide.

'We have the heir of David. He will take his place on the throne when the time comes.'

'He is not a pawn Jehoiada. He is a little boy whose entire family, except for me, has been murdered by his very own grandmother.'

'He is Yahweh's anointed.'

'Really? Jehu was Yahweh's anointed according to Elisha. Are you sure you do not just make these prophecies up to suit your own ambitions?'

'I did not prophesize Joash. I did not say I had. He is of the line and that is all I need to know.'

'He is my nephew, that is all *I* need to know.' Sheba moved to leave and Aron followed, Joash still giggling in his arms.

Chapter 33

Isaac entered the portico at the steps of the temple as Aron and Sheba left the vestibule. He took one look at the Princess's expression and wisely chose not to comment.

'We are leaving.' Sheba stormed past him with Aron close behind.

'Where are we going?' Isaac changed his mind, deciding that reason was likely in order.

'I do not care. As long as it is away from that, that traitor.'

'We have just received word from the palace.' The assassin decided that changing the subject would be far easier than dealing with this issue head on.

'What word?' Sheba stopped on the temple portico, the sun just reaching inside.

'It seems the Queen has sent a messenger, offering her hospitality in the palace.'

'What are her exact words?' Sheba tried to take the venom from her tone, but it was unsuccessful.

'She offers her utmost and sincere apology for any trauma the last day of events has caused. Further, she guarantees you have safe passage in the palace and it would be her honour to host you and your husband as her guests.'

'Do you think she knows?' The Princess turned to Aron who was still holding Joash.

'I doubt it. She likely wants something from Jehoiada and the only way to get that is to keep you alive. You remember your Grandmother's vision.'

'What vision?' Isaac asked before thinking better of it.

'A long story brother.' He returned his focus to the Princess. 'Marrying Jehoiada was one of the few messages she was absolutely sure of. Maybe this is why?'

Sheba's brow creased with her concern. 'You mean I have to stay with him? Oh Aron, I am not sure I can. Not now, knowing he is the reason my brother is dead.'

'He is not the reason Princess.' Isaac shrugged. 'Believe me, the last thing I want to do is defend the coward, but I was on a standing order to kill you or him. It was undecided for some time.'

'Why would Jehu want to kill Jehoiada if he aided him?' Aron rubbed his beard with his free hand and Joash copied the action with curiosity.

'Exactly!' Isaac waited for Sheba to comprehend what he was saying before carrying on. 'No doubt the Priest knew something was going to happen to the King or Kings but he serves only one master and it is not Jehu.'

'He thought this was Yahweh's doing?' Sheba's eyes grew wide with understanding. 'Why would anyone wish to believe that the God of Israel would want the Kings of Israel and Judah murdered?'

'We should ask him.' Aron offered.

'Because the Prophet Elisha ordained it. Who am I to argue with a prophet?' Jehoiada joined the conversation, having followed them through the vestibule to catch the end of the conversation.

'The Queen offers us an audience. What do you make of it?' Sheba asked her husband.

'Nothing good, of that I am sure. Yet, we can hardly decline, now can we?'

****

The smell of death still hung in the air as the small group entered the palace main gate. The walls had been scrubbed clean of blood and sawdust was laid over the gravel yard to soak up any remaining offensive marks.

'You will leave your weapons at the main hall.' The guard on duty nodded to another guard who waited inside, ready to disarm them.

'I am not sure about this.' Aron spoke under his breath to Isaac who shrugged casually.

'Weapons will do us no good in here today brother. Look around you.'

Aron did as Isaac instructed and he quickly understood his brother's statement. Guards lined the grand entrance with its mosaic floors and tall stone walls. Each passageway that led away into various parts of the palace was guarded by two sentries with sword and spear.

They were herded toward the main hall, where they could hear music and laughter. As they entered, it became obvious that the Queen was holding court, something Ahaziah had not chosen to do for years.

Dignitaries, courtiers, entertainers and beautiful maids were dancing and food and wine was flowing freely.

Sheba suddenly felt underdressed, having left the palace with only the tunic she escaped with. Thaliah saw the group enter and spoke to a servant who stood just behind her high-backed, regal chair.

The man bowed and rushed to meet the group. He bowed before the Princess. 'Your

Grace. The Queen suggests you and your friends might like to freshen up before you join the festivities. Your room is ready for you of course and your friends can...' He studied Isaac and Aron carefully. 'I will bring suitable attire for your friends.'

He looked at the High Priest who was dressed in his formal robes and smiled with approval. 'High Priest. Might you join the Queen while you await your wife and friends?'

Jehoiada's lips pursed as he considered the question, but he took the opportunity to make eye-contact with Sheba who nodded her agreement. His face lit up in a well-practised smile as he agreed to do just that.

The servant called another over to show the Priest to the Queen's table and then began to show the Princess to her room.

'No need. I have been here before. I know my way.' Sheba did not attempt to hide her frustration from the servant who was entirely unfamiliar to her.

'I am sorry your Grace. The Queen insisted you be accompanied at all times.' There was something in the man's eyes that made her feel uncomfortable, but she dismissed it as her paranoia.

'Very well.' She nodded as the man led the way to her familiar rooms. Memories of the night before flashed before her eyes and for a moment she felt unsteady. Aron reached for her arm but she frowned and pulled it away. The Queen did not need to know who Aron was to her. It would only put his life in danger.

'Here you are your Grace. Gentlemen, if you will follow me.' The servant bowed to the Princess and waited for Isaac and Aron to follow him.

'I do not mean any disrespect but I am the Princess's bodyguard, appointed by her uncle, before his most recent death and endorsed by her brother, before his untimely loss. She will not leave my sight.'

'But good sir. You cannot wait inside while she changes and you cannot change out here.'

'No. You are correct. We will wait out here until the Princess is ready. You can bring our clothing to us here and once the Princess has finished, I am sure she will not mind us utilising her room to make ourselves respectable.'

The servant seemed to pout like a contemptuous child, but decided in reality, it was a reasonable request. 'Very well. I will return shortly.'

'What do you make of all this?' Aron enquired as soon as the servant was out of earshot.

'If I were to guess, I believe that for whatever reason, Thaliah wants to appear like this massacre had nothing to do with her and that Sheba is her pride and joy—the only survivor.'

'It looks that way. She is likely pulling Jehoiada's strings as we speak, so let us return to the festivities as soon as possible,' Sheba said as she opened her door to enter her room.

The smell of jasmine flowers greeted her and her room had been tidied. Her clothes were laid out on her bed, as though the Queen had ordered she wear a particular dress this evening. The Princess placed it back in her cupboard and pulled out a more suitable option.

She pulled on the purple loose fitted pants and tied them around the waist. Over the top, she chose a cream coloured tunic with openings in the arms and pearl buttons at the wrist. She tied the tunic with a gold sash and quickly brushed and braided her hair. She smiled at the finished effect.

Over her face, she wore a sheer gold Hijab that draped around her neck and clipped closed on the other side.

She opened the door to find the servant had returned with two robes. She bit back the words that came to her mind as she recognised them as Ahaziah's.

As she moved out onto the veranda, Isaac went inside to change.

'You can both change together. We have held up the proceedings long enough gentlemen.' The servant seemed mildly agitated.

'I do not think so. As I said, I do not let the Princess out of my sight.' Aron took a deep breath and allowed his chest to expand as he drew himself up to his full height.

The servant rolled his eyes and once again, Sheba wondered who on earth he was.

'You are new, yes?' Sheba decided to ask her unanswered question. The man nodded. 'Where were you trained? Your manner is quite unusual for a palace servant, especially one as high ranking as you appear to be.'

'Needs must your Grace. I owned a tavern in the poor quarter. When I heard that there was work at the palace yesterday, I applied.'

'The news travelled awfully fast.' Sheba grinned as the servant shrugged.

Isaac opened the door and exited, as Aron entered. Sheba was stunned momentarily by their resemblance. The fact that they were brothers was suddenly blatantly obvious. Isaac had trimmed his beard significantly, in a similar way to Aron's. They were almost identical now, except for the colour of their eyes and hair.

'You should shave more often.' Sheba whispered and Isaac grinned in reply.

Aron opened the door and joined them once more. 'Shall we go?' He did not offer his arm to the Princess. Instead he and Isaac waited for her to lead and both followed at a respectful distance.

Chapter 34

Jehoiada pushed his food around his plate absentmindedly, while the Queen chatted as though the day before had never happened.

'How is married life treating you?' Jehoiada shook himself from his daydream as he realised the question required an answer.

'Very well thank you, your Grace.'

'Please! I prefer to be called your Highness.' The Queen smiled but it failed to reach her eyes. Jehoiada hesitated a moment before obliging the new monarch.

'Of course. *Your Highness*.' He nodded his head in a sitting bow.

'You seem tense. Is my step-daughter looking after you?' The Priest blushed at such a direct and personal question.

'It was a rather worrisome night. That is all.'

'Of course. I had no idea the Princess was in the palace when, well you know, when the ruckus broke out. I assumed she was with you, in the temple.' The question behind her statement was not missed on the Priest.

'Sheba and her bodyguard had returned to collect some more of her personal effects.'

'Yes. I had noticed she left quite a lot in her room in the palace. Why is that?'

'My room at the temple is that of a single man, your Highness. Sheba has been sleeping in the palace from time to time and enjoying a little of the luxury to which she is accustomed.'

'Of course.' The Queen looked sideways at the Priest and smiled. 'I wonder. Do you recall our discussion?' The Priest frowned at her vagueness. 'Before you married Sheba?'

'Yes.' Jehoiada returned his gaze to his meal and wrapped some vegetables into a flatbread, deciding eating was preferable to talking at this moment.

'I hope so.' All eyes moved to the entrance as the Princess and her two bodyguards entered the main hall. 'Ah. I see the Princess is ready to join us.' The tone was dry and a few scoffs and giggles from those close by accompanied the Queen's remark.

Sheba smiled without any hint of embarrassment. 'I do apologize Thaliah. It has been such a long few days. I am sure you understand.'

An audible gasp filled the room as many held their breath, awaiting the Queen's response. Thaliah nodded to her personal servant who refilled her cup with blood red wine and stepped back quickly.

'Please, do take a seat child.'

Aron escorted the Princess to the vacant seat next to the Queen, while Isaac leant against a pillar, his arms crossed over his chest and one foot resting against the pillar.

'Your guards can take a seat with my Captain of the guard.'

'Thank you Mother, but they will stand.' The Queen raised an eyebrow at her step-daughter. Sheba was unsure if it was due to the manner of address or her refusal of the meal for Aron and Isaac, but at this time, she did not care.

Aron touched her shoulder in warning, as he bowed and stepped back behind her chair. The servant who waited on the Queen's every command gave him a sideways glance, but wisely chose to say nothing.

The evening carried on into the late night with entertainment and frivolities for the wealthy dignitaries and guests. Just as Sheba was preparing to politely leave, the music stopped abruptly.

A line of Baal priests entered the palace hall, an eerie chant echoed around the walls. Their dark robes covered their heads as they carried a golden calf, surrounded by herbs and flowers, fruit and opium pipes.

'What is going on?' Sheba asked to anyone willing to answer.

Jehoiada looked as though he had seen a ghost as the Baal priests lowered their cargo amidst the dance floor. Guests moved back to give them room, looking at each other questioningly. Murmurs broke out throughout the hall but no-one moved.

'You are mine to command Priest, remember our deal.' Thaliah whispered to Jehoiada who gasped as half naked women ran into the room, dancing around the calf, throwing flower petals on the statue that depicted the false god Baal.

The assembled guests who were not in shock, clapped and hooted at the display, while Aron moved forward to offer Sheba his hand to stand.

'It has been a long day after a very long night. It is time to leave Jehoiada.' Sheba looked at her stepmother who only smiled condescendingly.

'No questions?' She offered sweetly.

'No. I will send someone for my belongings tomorrow and not trouble you again.'

'Not necessary daughter. You are welcome in the palace.'

'You honour me, but there is nothing left here for me now. My place is with my husband, in the house of Yahweh.'

'Your place is wherever I say it is.' The Queen spoke barely above a whisper before turning to the High Priest. 'And you will know when I call upon your service.'

'You seem to have all that under control your Highness. You have no need of me.' Jehoiada stood and joined his wife as Isaac fell into place behind Aron as the small group left the hall.

****

'What was that all about?' Sheba grumbled as the foursome sat in Jehoiada's small room.

'It was Thaliah's show of power.' Jehoiada moved the scrolls and paperwork from his blanket chest as he spoke, before offering Aron and Isaac a seat.

'I am surprised she let you walk out of there.' Isaac rubbed his chin, the new, shorter beard feeling strange to his touch.

'She needs Jehoiada.' Aron took the cup of water Jehoiada offered.

'What for? I will not denounce my faith.'

'She needs you to keep the temple running, so that there is something to offset her new regime,' Aron continued as Sheba and Jehoiada both frowned.

'That makes no sense. Why not just eliminate us?'

'The Zealots would come down on her and her kingdom like wild fire. She needs time to build her army, her loyal followers and what better way to do that, than with gold, power, the promise of unjudged promiscuity? You saw the faces of most of the men there tonight.'

'Not very many men turn away from free rutting with whoever they want,' Isaac chuckled to himself 'especially if the Queen is offering power and prestige with it.'

'She will corrupt the entire kingdom.' Jehoiada was ghostly white once more.

'I believe that is her plan and keeping you alive, and happy,' Aron pointed to Sheba, 'is Thaliah's way of making sure the Zealots stay away, otherwise Jehu would be here already.'

'So I will send word and he will come.' Jehoiada jumped to his feet, suddenly believing he had the answer to all his worries.

'And what then?' Aron's question left the Priest confused.

'The Zealots will restore Joash to the throne.'

'They might.' Aron offered but looked to his brother for guidance.

'I doubt it.' Isaac offered after more thought. 'Jehu is power hungry. He would likely kill Sheba just for her blood line, then control Joash as his regent or kill him and take control of Judah.'

'Oh!' Jehoiada sat down heavily. 'I can see politics is not my strong point after all.'

'So, we let her rule Judah, corrupting our citizens and ruining what is left of my family's honour?' Sheba's face was one of defeat and Aron wanted nothing more but to take her in his arms, but he could not.

'No Princess, we raise Joash until he is old enough to take the throne. We use this time to gain favour with the army generals. Both Isaac and I know many of them.' Aron looked to Isaac for support.

'Where else am I to go?' He smiled and gave a small nod. 'Jehu will know of my deceit by now.'

'Deceit?' Jehoiada's brow creased.

'Yes. Isaac was supposed to kill Sheba for Jehu—another reason we know it is unwise to expect any help from him.' Aron patted the Priest on the shoulder in consolation.

'So the Priest becomes the spy.' Isaac laughed and everyone joined in.

Chapter 35

Sheba watched Joash playing with a small group of children in a laneway, not far from the marketplace.

'Your Grace.' A young woman, much the same age as Sheba with the same almost black eyes and shining black hair smiled as she tapped Sheba on the shoulder.

'Leah. I have told you, you must call me Sheba.' The girl curtsied and giggled nervously. 'Come, sit. This is important.' The Princess patted the space on the stone wall next to her.

'You understand why I employed you?' The woman nodded. 'I have enemies and you are here to not only help me run my household, but to confuse those who might be watching me.'

'I am sorry, Sheba.' She smiled at the Princess's approving nod. 'It is not that I do not understand my role. It is that you are a Princess.' The girl whispered so no-one could hear except Sheba. 'I am still a little nervous. I will get better, I promise.'

'Thank you. I am sure that you will. Now collect Joash for me, as though he were your very own. We will take him back inside the house.'

The young woman collected the giggling toddler up in her arms and swung him around like a proud mother would. 'You darling boy. Come, let us wash your dirty face.' She spat on her finger and wiped a spot of jam from the boy's top lip.

Sheba smiled as Leah carried him into her new home.

'You stay with the baby and I will visit my husband. Now you remember the rules. We will pay you well, but you will not use a name in public when you refer to the boy.' The girl nodded. 'His life depends on it.' She nodded more vigorously.

'I will make your meal, Sheba.' Leah smiled. 'Did you want me to cook for Aron and Isaac?'

Sheba smiled to herself. 'Yes, that would be a good idea.' Leah had grown quite smitten with Isaac after he found her in the local tavern. She was a terrible waitress, but the perfect double for the Princess. It would become more and more difficult for Thaliah's spies to tell them apart, making it easier for Sheba to hug and teach her nephew as he grew.

****

'Already, she is persecuting Yahweh's people.' Jehoiada wrung his hands.

'What do you mean?' Aron asked as Sheba entered her husband's office.

'Her guards tossed their market stalls and beat two men of Yahweh's temple today, pious men, who visit the temple to pray daily and offer their generosity to the running of this establishment.'

'You mean they pay you?' Isaac chuckled.

'Well, yes. But that is not the point. Thaliah is targeting them, to create fear. Her guards painted the outside of the temple walls with terrible writings and pictures of Baal.'

'It is all harmless Priest. It is just to frighten people.'

'Well it is working.' Jehoiada protested. 'You mark my words, in years to come we will be facing poverty if she is not stopped.'

'Is the gold all that worries you man?' Isaac shook his head.

'No, but poor people follow whoever offers to feed them. Yahweh will lose many, I promise you.'

There was silence a moment as Jehoiada composed himself. Sheba placed a cast-pot of stew on the Priest's desk and began ladling it out into bowls.

'If Yahweh's people lose faith so quickly husband, I challenge they never had it to begin with.'

'They are only sheep Princess.' Isaac offered in Jehoiada's defence. 'They are easily led.'

'Leah is looking after Joash.' She decided to change the subject. There was no limit to how long Thaliah's reign would go on and therefore no point in harping on about her deeds.

'How are you finding your new home?' Aron asked as he moved to take two bowls from the Princess. One he took to Jehoiada who raised an eyebrow but nodded his thanks.

'Much better than trying to run such a ruse in the lodgings provided in the temple.' She smiled. 'I cannot believe you found someone who looks so much like me.' The Princess took a bowl to Isaac who reached out to take it, a smile making him look mischievous.

'She is not a patch on the real thing, but pretty to look at.' Sheba blushed, but quickly composed herself when she saw both Aron and Jehoiada's expressions.

'How long do we have to continue this?' She looked to the High Priest for an answer.

'We will know when the time is right.' Isaac answered. 'Aron and I will leave soon to find allies, those loyal to the line of David, not the Zealots and not Thaliah.'

'You will need to take letters to the Levites.' Jehoiada put his bowl down and began looking for parchment. 'I will need to write them.'

'There is plenty of time Priest. Eat your meal. We will make a list of all the Priests, Levites and Generals who will be favourable to the line of David.'

'Yes, but you cannot tell them of Joash outright. Any one of them could be a spy for Thaliah.' Sheba protested.

'We will be careful. That is why this could take years.'

'We need time to train Joash in any case.' Jehoiada rubbed his long beard as he considered the boy's education. 'He must not fall into the trap of his father.'

'What trap?' Sheba spoke with a mouthful of stew and Aron suddenly grinned, recalling another night.

'Worshipping Baal.'

'Ahaziah did not worship Baal. He believed in Yahweh. He told me so himself.'

'Well complacency is the same as worshipping. It is because of Jehoram and

Ahaziah that the Baal religion grew strong enough to do what they are doing now.'

Sheba started collecting up the empty bowls and snatched Jehoiada's, still only half eaten. 'My brother only ever wanted peace and for his people to be free to choose who they believe in. Blind faith is not the way of a King. Not the way of an educated man and I do not believe the way of Yahweh either.'

The Princess stormed out of the office leaving all three men open mouthed. Isaac began to clap slowly and both Aron and Jehoiada looked at him quizzically.

'You should have stuck to matters of faith Priest, because when it comes to women, you have no idea.' Isaac stood and left, followed shortly by Aron who could not stop grinning stupidly.

Isaac looked over his shoulder and waited for Aron to catch up. 'She might have killed him by the time we get back.'

'With any luck.' Aron laughed.

Chapter 36

'Do you think they know?' Anath whispered, looking around her nervously.

'We will not speak of it sister. Moloch has an uncanny ability to listen in when I have no idea he is around.'

'Did he have anything to do with that display in the palace? The Baal priests? That was heavy handed, even for him.' Astarte adjusted her leather girdle, her ample bosom bulging in the process.

'Do you mind?' Anath poked Astarte's chest, 'Contain those things.'

'You are just jealous?' Astarte laughed.

'I can have them too.' Anath changed her appearance and both Goddesses giggled like maidens.

'You two behave.' Asherah grumbled good-naturedly. 'Jerusalem is in for a tumultuous time under Thaliah's rule. I would say Baal has everything to do with this. He has found favour once more and he is not about to waste it.'

'Gabriel and Michael would say it is all part of Father's plan.' Anath changed back to her blonde, lean self as she spoke.

'It might be, but we need to focus on our plan. Anath, Astarte, follow Aron and Isaac. I will watch over our Princess.' Asherah disappeared.

'I think we could have a lot of fun watching over those two.' Astarte smiled and Anath pondered the idea without any seriousness.

'One is very close to the Princess,' she winked.

'Yes, but who can resist a Goddess?' Astarte pushed her bosom up with both hands once more as she too disappeared.

****

'You have changed Mattan. Thaliah took the bottle of elixir offered and pulled the stopper with her teeth. The Priest watched as she licked the top with her tongue and savoured the flavour.

'And you also, your Highness.' Mattan's eyes flashed with a sparkle Thaliah had not seen before, as he opened her robe and ran his fingertips down her naked body.

She shivered and placed the vial in her mouth, swallowing the liquid in one hurried mouthful. Mattan's lips were all over hers before she could take a breath and for a moment, she felt as though she might faint.

'I thought Priests took a vow of chastity?' Thaliah stroked Mattan's hair as his lips lingered on her neck.

'Not Baal priests.' He lifted the Queen by her buttocks as she wrapped her legs around his hips. She felt the cold of the stone altar as he placed her down, his hips in line with hers.

Mattan licked her nipple and she opened her eyes. The temple was full to overflowing with men and women of her court. She shuddered, not sure if it was the power or the excitement as Mattan's lips moved down over her belly button and beyond.

****

Moloch has seen enough. The earthly pleasures had never been of interest to him. Baal was in his element now. Taking the form of the priest and enjoying what angels had always been forbidden was likely to catch the eye of the Archangels.

This was what caused the fall of his brethren. Humans were a distraction, a temptation set by their father to test them and always, so many failed the test.

He opened his wings and moved up through the veil like a shooting star. He had a war to win and now that the line was broken, the Redeemer would be lost. Maybe now, his father would listen to reason.

Chapter 37

Sheba ruffled Joash's dark curly hair as he rushed through the hallway to the cookhouse table beyond. She shook her head as she heard him excitedly asking her husband question after question as he prepared for his morning lessons.

He had grown so quickly from the toddler they had saved from near death, to the vivacious boy with an insatiable appetite for learning.

She collected a bucket of water from the outside trough and made her way back to help Leah.

'So, you see now Joash. See what the Baal priests have done?' Jehoiada schooled the future King as Sheba stopped to listen, chewing her lip to keep herself from interrupting.

Joash waited on every word his uncle uttered with uncharacteristic patience.

'Now, tell me why Yahweh is almighty and why we should not worship the gods of the unworthy.'

'Because Yahweh fed our ancestors in the desert, gave them the commandments and helped them win the promised land. This land.'

Sheba shook her head, her patience evaporating. 'Joash, it is time you cleaned up for your morning meal. You have more important education to pursue, your numbers, your letters.'

The boy jumped to his feet and ran past Leah and out of the cook room. 'You must stop it Jehoiada.' Sheba waited until her nephew was outside, washing his hands in the yard sink.

'Nonsense. How is he to know right from wrong when he… when the time comes?' Jehoiada looked at Leah, who continued to prepare the meal, yet her ears were open to the bickering that was going on around her.

'I understand he must know Yahweh, but do you have to make him ignorant of the beliefs of others? There are many tribes who live in Jerusalem. He should not think them any lesser people than his own.'

'Why not? Yahweh gave *us* the promised land, not the Canaanites, not the Hittites, *us*!'

'Yes and he told us to be stewards over it, not kill everyone that did not agree with *us*.'

Leah left the room to fetch Joash for his meal.

'That is not the lesson from the story of Jericho. Yahweh turned the walls to rubble to kill all the pagans within.'

'That is your interpretation. Others say not all perished inside the walls and that Jacob was not doing the work of Yahweh but following his own agenda, for his own pride.'

'The Kings of Israel and Judah are to follow Yahweh and only Him. They are not to tolerate the worship of false idols. It is written.'

Sheba sighed. Men were so arrogant. The Priest took his wife's silence as a sign of her resignation.

'The time is near Sheba. The Levites and Priests have been invited to the ceremony.' He fell silent as Leah returned.

'You do not think that after six years of looking after Joash, the woman has not discovered who he is? You can be such a fool Jehoiada. Leah! Come, sit with us.' The Princess smiled and Leah returned the gesture, trying to not find her master's bickering so enjoyable.

'Now, continue Jehoiada, Leah will need to know what is going on with your most complex plan.'

Joash rushed back in, pulled up a stool to the table and began shovelling food into his mouth, oblivious to the conversation going on around him. Jehoiada was so distracted, he failed to insist the boy give thanks to Yahweh before eating.

'Aron and Isaac have done well.' Leah blushed at the mention of Isaac's name and Sheba patted her hand, understanding passing between them.

'So what are your plans when you name Joash King?' Jehoiada frowned at the Princess's openness, but it would be common knowledge soon.

'We will have the backing of the Levites and enough of the army of Judah to overthrow Thaliah. We'll burn the temple of Baal to the ground and kill all the heathens who worship there.'

'Kill the heathens.' Joash muttered between mouthfuls of food. Sheba turned pale as she clenched her fists.

'What have you done Jehoiada? This journey,' she pointed to Joash, 'started with a massacre. You cannot seriously think it is Yahweh's will to end it with another?'

'History says that it is Yahweh's will... the fall, the flood, Jericho. When Yahweh wishes his people to prosper, the death of His enemies must ensue.'

'You have gone mad. You have joined the Zealots while I was not looking. Most of the people you speak of do what Thaliah wishes from fear. You will make their fears a reality.'

'It is Yahweh's will.' Jehoiada stood and moved to sit with Joash as if the conversation were over.

'I am so glad I have never given you a child. It is bad enough my nephew has been corrupted by your bigoted thinking, no child of mine will ever be damaged in such a way.'

Sheba left her home with tears in her eyes. She did not know where she was going to go, but her heart ached and her limbs were moving without any thought.

She thought about going to the temple, but at that moment, she was too angry with Yahweh to even contemplate a prayer to Him. She walked through the alleyways that led to the forest beyond the walls of Jerusalem.

Aron was away again and she knew he would be so angry with her leaving the city without his protection, but right now, she was too furious to care. No-one paid her any mind now; she was nothing more than the forgotten princess.

The Princess found a grove of oak trees surrounded by a blanket of red poppies. She sat down amongst the shaded blooms and pulled her legs up under her robe. She had held her tears in check all the way from her home, but now, as she buried her head in her hands, she finally gave way to the waves of sobs. She was unsure how long she had been there, but long enough to feel exhaustion setting in.

'Child. You do not need to cry.' Sheba recognised the bell-like tone of the Goddess and looked to see her radiant body through her tear streaked vision.

'It was all for nothing.' Sheba wiped her running nose on the sleeve of her tunic and used the back of her hand to try and wipe away the tears.

Asherah moved closer, wrapping her arm around the still young and beautiful Princess. The last few years had aged her only a little, but her eyes looked older than the Goddess wished to know.

'What was for nothing?'

'My destiny. All for nothing. I sacrificed a life with Aron, away from this madness. You told me I would make a difference.'

'Aron has stayed with you Princess and you have known the love of a strong man, but yes, you have made sacrifices. But not for nothing.'

'Yes, for nothing. Jehoiada has indoctrinated Joash right before my eyes and the poor child has no idea he is to be used as a pawn in a religious struggle for power.'

'It does not matter who wins or loses this struggle, the battle has already been won.' The

Princess looked like she was ready to hit the Goddess, but she held her temper in check.

'Hundreds will die Asherah and it is my fault.'

'It is not your fault child.' Asherah wondered how much she could tell the Princess. 'A Redeemer is written, in the texts of Israel. He is of King David's line. That was your destiny, to save Joash, to save the Redeemer's line. He is to bring peace to your people, to all Yahweh's people.'

'If the ancient writings are correct, we are all Yahweh's people. The Canaanites, the Hittites, the Amalekites, even the Philistines, we all came from the first man and the first woman. Right?' The Goddess nodded.

'So if we are all Yahweh's people then why do some, like Jehoiada and Jehu, think those of Israel and Judah are more valuable than those of other nations?'

'Because they are human. Your people see the Father as they would see themselves in His role, Lord over all, King of humanity, King of Heaven. They think with human hearts and human minds, but they do not understand how Father thinks. None of us does.'

'Then, if even you, the Angels do not know, we are doomed. Joash will reign fire on

all of Jerusalem and he will have no idea what
he is doing.'

Chapter 38

Sheba waited to ensure her husband had gone to the temple before she returned home. For a moment, she had considered taking Joash away but then realised, without Aron and Isaac, the chances of getting far were slim.

'Are you alright Sheba?' Leah jumped to her feet as soon as the Princess entered the room. 'Come, sit. You need something to eat.' The maid placed a bowl of warmed oats on the table and pointed for her mistress to sit before joining her.

'I will be fine. I am sorry to leave you with Jehoiada. He would have been in a foul mood after I left.' The Princess spooned a mouthful of food, suddenly realising how hungry she was.

'He finished his meal and left shortly after you. He took Joash with him.'

Sheba swallowed her mouthful of oats and smiled. 'He must read minds now,' she mumbled almost to herself.

'Your husband seemed very distressed and Joash did not want to go with him. He was quite upset when he saw you leave so suddenly.'

'It is a lot for a seven-year-old to understand. So much has changed over the past six years. Jehoiada was always a coward and had been a traitor to my brother, but he is very bitter. I realise that now.'

'You can understand why. The people of his temple have been terrorised. Even yourself, when those men of the Baal temple thought they could have their way with you.'

'Yes, I was lucky to have Aron and Isaac to watch over me.

'You were, we all are.' Leah blushed once more but quickly changed the subject. 'What I mean to say, it that it is as though the Queen has wiped your family from Judah's history.'

'I know she would like to, but not while I still draw breath.'

'The High Priest is afraid, afraid that your stepmother will do the same to Yahweh, that He will become nothing more than a distant memory.'

Sheba nodded her understanding. 'You are very wise for one so young.' The Princess patted Leah's hand, which was now on top of hers.

'No mistress, I have just seen from the outside, what you have both endured for these past years.'

'Thank you.' Sheba took a deep breath and stood. 'As hard as it is for me to admit, Joash must take his place on the throne. I just pray Yahweh is with him, for what Jehoiada plans to do, will leave him with nightmares to last a lifetime.'

****

Isaac opened the front door and held it for Aron.

'We are home.' Isaac called as he moved down the hallway to the main cookroom beyond. He barely opened the door before Leah was upon him.

'What took you so long? You have missed so much. There was a huge argument this morning.' Isaac pulled Leah to him and silenced her with his lips.

Aron and Sheba stood apart, their eyes on the couple who had forgotten they were not alone. Aron cleared his throat and Isaac looked up, his lips still pressed to Leah's.

'You need a room?' Aron offered.

'If you have one available.' Isaac grinned mischievously and Leah giggled.

'Sorry.' She curtsied and blushed in unison.

'No need. I can imagine the feeling.' Sheba smiled but it faded quickly.

Isaac looked from Aron to the Princess as he spoke. 'Come Leah, I think I can afford to treat you to a meal.' He put his arm around her waist and almost lifted her from the room.

'Wait, I need to get my hijab.' She reached for her scarf and hastily wrapped it around her neck and head before following Isaac from the building.

'They make a cute couple.' Aron poured a watered wine from the jug on the cooking bench, before sitting down and tapping the seat beside him. 'I assume we are alone?'

Sheba nodded and joined him, pouring herself a wine and sighing after the first mouthful slid down her throat.

'What did I miss?' Aron's eyes burrowed into Sheba's, searching for the cause of her anxiety.

'Jehoiada has made the final arrangements.'

'That is good news. I thought you would be happy?' Aron took a sip of his wine.

'I wish it were. He told me this morning what he plans to do once Joash takes the throne and I am not sure I want to bear witness.'

Aron waited patiently, knowing the Princess would share more once she was ready.

'He is going to kill all the Baal priests, the Queen, everyone that has not remained faithful to Yahweh. I am afraid we will be unleashing another massacre upon Jerusalem.'

Aron put his arm around the Princess and hugged her to his chest. She held back the tears, but him being so close made it all the more difficult to remain composed.

'What do you want to do?' Aron waited, brushing the Princess's hair through his fingers as she took another deep breath.

'I had considered taking Joash away, but he must take the throne. Asherah told me as much.'

'You saw the Goddess?'

'Yes.' Sheba pulled away to look at Aron. 'She told me I have fulfilled my destiny. That once Joash takes the throne it will be done. She explained more but I am not supposed to share it.'

'I understand.' Aron did not push her. Just knowing that Goddesses existed was enough to make the soldier understand some things were not for him to know or understand.

'I want to tell you, but I cannot.' Sheba's voice ached with concern.

'I told you. I understand. What I do want to know though, is what do *you* want to do? Whatever you decide, I am with you. Fight, take Joash and run, stay and become the aunt to the King...'

'Part of me hopes that I can influence Joash as he grows, but he is already so manipulated to Jehoiada's will, I am not sure I can break that spell.'

'How long before the ceremony?'

'A week, possibly more. Jehoiada will announce it as soon as he knows everyone is on the way to Jerusalem.'

Aron nodded and drew the Princess in to another embrace.

'I have missed you.'

'I missed you, more than you can understand. Thank you.'

'What for?' Aron breathed into Sheba's ear and the Priestess shivered with the sensation.

'For staying, when you could have found a wife and family elsewhere.'

'Without you, nothing else would matter Sheba.'

Chapter 39

Aron and Isaac scrubbed the temple stairs clean, their shirtless torsos running with sweat. They drew the looks of many, as they helped prepare for the ceremony.

'Passover is the perfect time to host such a large ceremony. The Queen will have no idea what is truly planned.' Jehoiada smiled at his ingenious idea.

'Spring is also a traditional time for other ceremonies. She may be upset you did not invite her.' Sheba wondered aloud.

'Orgies and howling at the moon.' Jehoiada shivered at the thought. 'The woman is an abomination. Those are not ceremonies, they are wicked, evil, depravities.'

'I agree she has taken the traditions too far. There is a great deal of corruption in Jerusalem, with all those who follow her. But not all who follow the traditional religion of this region are corrupt or depraved Jehoiada. Why do you feel you have the right to judge them?'

The Princess knew she was fighting a losing battle, but she hoped in her heart that Jehoiada would see truth in her words.

His face grew red as the veins on his temples pulsed with suppressed rage. 'I provide for you, love you and what do I get? Not your loyalty, that is for sure.'

The Princess wanted to argue, but she did not have the energy left. She wanted to tell him that he never loved her, only the prestige of marrying a Princess and with no royal heir, she had failed to meet his high expectations.

'I will help with the cleaning.' The Princess left Jehoiada, his mouth open, ready for another tirade. She had never loved him. She had not honoured him either, but her conscience was clear. She took a deep breath to compose herself before helping with the rest of the preparations.

'Sheba.' Joash called as he and Leah walked toward the temple. Leah stopped at the gates, knowing she was forbidden from entering. The boy carried on, oblivious.

'What are you doing here?' Sheba looked around nervously, a habit she had never shaken. Six years had passed, and not once had anyone questioned the façade they had created.

Joash had called Leah mother his entire life. To him, Sheba and Jehoiada were his mother's relatives, who helped provide food and care for him. What would happen when he discovered the truth? The Princess pushed the thought away.

'Jehoiada said I should come for a fitting? I am not sure what that is, but it sounds like fun.' The boy hopped from one foot to the other.

'Then you had best not hold the High Priest up. He is in the temple.' Sheba pointed the way and Joash stopped to give her a hug before skipping past her.

'His carefree days are soon at an end.' Sheba jumped as Aron spoke, just against her ear.

'Sorry. I did not mean to frighten you.' Aron grinned mischievously.

'Yes, you did.' Sheba returned the smile.

'That is much better. You are even more beautiful when you smile.'

****

'Where are all these people going?' Thaliah asked her Captain of the guard as he reported on the large number of Priests and Yahweh Zealots entering the city.

'A festival of some sort, in the temple.' The guard shrugged 'Passover or something like that.'

'Yes. That makes sense. But why such a big event? Why so many damned Priests? Get me Mattan!'

The Captain bowed and sauntered from the throne room.

'Now!' The Queen bellowed behind him, causing him to hasten his search for the Baal priest.

Thaliah was just about to start throwing things as Mattan entered the throne room.

She puzzled over the man. He was often vague, to say the least and then he would suddenly become quite demanding and even frightening. It was always this side that the Queen enjoyed most.

Today, as he entered, she watched closely, to see how he would react to the flow of Zealot Priests entering Baal's domain.

'You *demanded* my presence?' The Queen smiled. No bow, no title, a touch of sardonic flavour. This was her favourite version of the man.

'Have you been asleep all day?' She smirked as Mattan's eyebrow rose, almost saying *Challenge accepted!*

'Possibly. It was a rather tiring night last night. I needed my beauty sleep. What is happening that could possibly be so urgent?'

'Priests and not Baal priests are flooding into Jerusalem. Something is happening and *you* should know about it.'

Mattan frowned. Moloch had given him no forewarning, in fact, he had not seen Moloch for months, or was it years? Time was fleeting for the angelic.

'Are you still intoxicated or something?' The Queen tapped her booted foot on the stone dais and scowled. Mattan only grinned which further served to frustrate Thaliah.

'I was just considering why my spies or yours had not reported anything?'

'Probably because they have become lazy, over indulged bureaucratic pigs?'

'You make that sound as though it is my fault. It is you who insisted on bringing them to the temple to be indulged.' Mattan approached the throne and Thaliah did not protest. 'You look like you are stressed. Let me help you with that.'

Thaliah took a deep breath to relax as Mattan knelt before the Queen, running his hands up the inside of her legs, without lifting her skirt.

She looked to the guards at her side and tipped her head for them to leave. They were well versed in royal etiquette and moved without a backward glance. As tantalizing as the sounds were, no-one wanted to be executed for witnessing the Queen's *rituals* without permission.

 **Chapter 40**

The women lined the outside wall, all craning to get a glimpse of the proceedings. The courtyard was completely full of Levites, Priests and any male worshipper who wished to attend the Passover festival.

Leah and Isaac waited outside the gates together, observing the pomp and ceremony with mixed emotions.

'This is going to be a long day.' Leah smiled as Isaac wrapped his arms around her waist and she rested the back of her head against his chest.

'We could skip out for a little while and come back for the finale if you like?'

'I am feeling so nervous for Joash.' Isaac smiled at the boy's nursemaid. She had brought him up as her own child for so long, he knew her heart was about to break when he became the new King.

'Are you planning on following him to the palace?' Isaac whispered, his chin against her ear.

Leah shook her head. 'No, that will be Sheba's role, not mine.'

Isaac breathed in the smell of her lavender scented hair and took a deep breath, finding the courage he needed. 'Then, would you like to leave Jerusalem with me?'

Leah spun around, wrapped her hands around Isaac's neck and kissed him before realising the combined eyes of every gathered woman were suddenly burrowing into her with contempt.

'Ignore them. Where we go, no-one will judge you for being yourself.'

The woman next to the assassin tusked loudly and Isaac's expression grew stern. She averted her eyes as the couple continued to kiss.

'I would love to go where you go.' Leah turned back to watch the parade of Priests, with incense pots and long sparkling robes as they began the procession into the temple.

'I only hope this goes as smoothly as the Priest thinks.' Isaac muttered almost to himself. He touched the hilt of his sword reflexively as he nodded to the eagle-eyed men, just inside the gates.

****

'I am scared.' Joash hugged Sheba around the neck as she struggled to gently release his hands so she could stand.

'You are going to be a king Joash. You do not need to feel afraid of anything. Yahweh will be with you.'

'I never wanted to be a king. I still do not understand.' The boy pouted and Sheba was reminded once more that he was only a little boy.

'I know it is hard Joash. I am still your aunt and Jehoiada really is your uncle.'

'And my mother is dead?' The little boy was close to tears now.

'Leah is still your mother Joash, just not the one who gave birth to you. She died when you were born.' Sheba knelt back down, suddenly torn with her decision to go ahead with the ordination.

'It is time Joash.' Jehoiada walked into the vestibule dressing room and grabbed the boy gently, but firmly on the shoulder.

Joash looked pleadingly at the Princess, who kissed his forehead, took a deep breath to compose herself and then stood to allow her husband to take him.

She watched the little boy leave, after a backward glance, then he was gone from sight, just before the tears began to fall.

A pair of arms embraced her and she fell into them. 'Why? Why would Yahweh want a boy to become a king?'

'Maybe He does not.' Aron wiped a tear from Sheba's cheek as he kissed her forehead.

'But Asherah said it was his destiny.'

'It likely is. But it is Jehoiada's choice to make this happen now. He will be the real king.'

Sheba gasped. Why had she not realised this before? 'I have been so stupid.'

'No, you have never been stupid Sheba. Jehoiada probably does not even know it is power he seeks. It is the way of men.'

'He will have free reign over Joash after today.' She bit her lip. 'I am sorry.'

'Why?' Aron kissed the Princess once more before she pulled away and smoothed her dress, suddenly realising if anyone had walked in, she would have put both their lives at risk.

'I must stay... to protect Joash.'

'No-one can protect Joash now except Yahweh. You have a choice to make. How deep is your faith?'

'What do you mean?'

'You can stay and I have already said, if that is what you choose, I will be here, with you. But if Yahweh is truly with Joash, then He will protect the boy.'

'But me staying could be Yahweh's way of protecting him.' Sheba sighed.

'Then the choice I guess is really a case of, do you believe you deserve happiness? Or a life of servitude?

'Well that is the thing Aron,' she touched his cheek gently and smiled wistfully, 'I was born into servitude. I was destined to always be a token bride, to broker a treaty of one sort or another. This is just another treaty.'

Aron's lips turned into a sad smile. 'You know, this is why I love you so much.'

The sound of music broke their solitude and Aron nodded for the Princess to go first. He followed her from the dressing-room into the vestibule at a respectable distance for a bodyguard.

The ceiling was huge, but the vestibule was not very large. It marked the entrance to the temple holy place, where the boy would soon become the King.

A select group of Priests and Levites now occupied the temple. Sheba was the only woman present and Aron watched the quizzical gazes fall on her, making her fidget nervously.

He did not hide his disdain, which caused most Priests to direct their gaze back at the boy, who now stood at the altar. Behind him, in the most Holy of Holies, between the two giant winged lion statues that marked where no man could go, stood the Ark of the Covenant of Yahweh.

The walls of the temple were lined with gold, casting light from bronze mirrors that were mounted high, to catch the light from the few openings. The Ark glowed, not with the same light as the walls, but with a light that no-one could explain.

The sound of the Priests chanting filled the temple, and travelled beyond the walls like a wave.

'You know why you are here. You have been chosen to bear witness to the renewing of our covenant with Yahweh. Once more, a descendent of David will sit upon the throne.'

The Priests continued to chant as Jehoiada took a golden circle from the altar and placed it on Joash's head. The boy looked frightened and Aron could see Sheba fighting the urge to protect him. He looked at her, still pleading for his nightmare to end, but she smiled and blew him a kiss. He returned the gesture with a shy smile.

As soon as the golden circle was upon his head, the chanting stopped. Jehoiada took the boy by the arm and led him from the temple, to the vestibule and the steps that led down to the courtyard.

'Today is not just any Passover festival. Today!' Jehoiada waited for all eyes to settle on him and silence to fill the courtyard below. 'Today is the day Yahweh has restored his promise, his covenant with his people.'

People murmured softly and looked to each other for understanding.

'Today I give you King Joash, son of Ahaziah, true heir to the throne of Judah.'

A cheer rose from the courtyard. Those outside the gate had not fully heard the announcement, but men within quickly told their wives and friends what had happened. The sound of cheering became louder, roaring like a thunderstorm.

'Now it begins.' Aron moved closer to the Princess and whispered directly in her ear. 'Now we need to get Joash to safety.'

Chapter 41

'What is going on out there?' Thaliah's dark red curtains were drawn shut. Arms and legs were tangled all over her bed as the Queen unthreaded herself to discover the source of the roaring and cheering outside.

She could barely open her eyes to the daylight beyond, feeling the throbbing of her head from the night before. 'Someone tell me what is going on?'

A servant rushed into the room, a fresh pitcher of water in his hand and his eyes downcast to avoid seeing the Queen's nakedness. She held her cup low in front of him and glared as he poured her a goblet, which she drank greedily. 'Find me someone who can tell me what all that noise is about.'

The servant bowed and backed from the room, averting his eyes as two naked bodies sat up and stretched.

Thaliah watched the two young men get out of bed and smiled. Her life was almost perfect she thought, until the sound of roaring forced her to peer out the window once more.

The temple was overflowing with people. The women outside were dancing with one another. The men within were cheering and back slapping as though they had all been granted unlimited riches.

She strained to see from the palace exactly what all the celebration was about, but she grumbled to herself for letting Mattan distract her from finding out what the temple Priests were up to. A sinking feeling in her stomach told her it was not good.

She dressed, splashed her face with water and called for a servant to fix her make up. By the time she left her apartment and took her seat on the throne, Mattan had arrived.

He looked pale as he bowed before her. Today she was faced with the boring, fastidious Priest, not her brazen favourite.

'What is all the commotion out there Mattan?' The Queen tapped her foot and waited. The Priest looked around, trying to decide if he should talk or run.

'I, I have only heard snippets of information on my way here your, your,' *What was the term she liked?* He felt so vague today, like he had drunk too much wine.

'Highness.' Thaliah coaxed, rolling her eyes. It was as though the man were losing his mind. It happened to the elderly, but Mattan was not an old man. She smiled at the thought of his smooth, rippling chest and then suddenly shook her head back to reality.

'The talk is….it cannot be right your Highness.'

'Just spit it out Mattan. I do not have all day. The crowd is getting noisy and I need to tell my guards what is happening.

'They say a new king has been crowned. Ordained by Yahweh, anointed by Jehoiada, high priest of the temple.'

'Why is this the first we are hearing about it? What of your spies? We talked about this yesterday. You assured me you were looking into it.' If Thaliah could have spat fire, she would have in that moment.

'We did?' The man looked positively pained. 'My memory.' He shook his head.

'Call the Captain of the guard. We need to find the source of this vicious rumour.'

Mattan did not move, he was still shaking his head to remove the fog that kept creeping into his mind. Images of the Queen, naked, filled his mind and he blushed, not really understanding where he could have seen such an image.

'Sit down Mattan. You looked like you are about to faint.' Thaliah growled and pointed to a chair at the side of the throne.

The two guards grinned at one another and quickly wiped away the expression as the Queen looked at the one on her left.

The throne room doors burst open as the Captain of the guard ran into the room. 'It is a riot your Highness.'

'Take a breath man. Explain yourself.' Thaliah sat forward on her throne.

'The people are rioting. My guards are hard pressed to keep the people from the palace.'

'What are you saying?' The Queen rolled her thumbs around one another nervously. 'We are under attack?'

'Soon. We will be soon. You need to make some sort of announcement. Calm the mob before it is too late.'

'Calm them with what?'

'I do not know. Coin, food. Anything.'

'Collect my counsel. They must be able to calm the people down. That *is* what I pay them for.'

'They are gone your Highness. I saw most of those bureaucratic phonies, with their wagons stacked high leaving early this morning, as soon as the festival began.'

'And you did not think to detain them, ask them why or maybe warn me?'

'I was a little busy. Have you seen the size of that crowd out there? And there is something else.'

'What!' Thaliah threw her hands in the air.

'There are armed men in that crowd. Not merchants with daggers, trained soldiers.'

'And you are only telling me this now?'

'I only just discovered it. They kept the weapons hidden, but when the crowd began marching on the palace, the weapons came out.'

Thaliah shook her head, trying to force herself to think clearly. 'Sheba. She must know what is going on. Find her. Now!'

'There is no point in me dragging the Princess here your Highness. By the time we find her, the mob will have taken the palace. I suggest you go find her.'

'You dare.' The Queen stood and stomped her foot. She puffed herself up and scowled, ready to release an onslaught of abuse on her Captain.

'Your choice. Live or die. I suggest you get off your backside and go find Sheba because if you do not work out what is going on soon, you are going to find yourself over-run with common people who, to be honest, do not really like you.' The man shrugged as he announced what most had been thinking for some time.

The Captain turned on his heel and ran from the throne room, the two guards stood open mouthed beside Thaliah, whose fist had turned white from a lack of blood flow.

'You two. With me.' She stood and left the throne room, both guards clamoured to catch up.

Chapter 42

Isaac moved forward as the Queen's guard began to advance on the crowd who were chanting *Long live the King! Long live the King!*

He and Aron had managed to find two generals loyal to Ahaziah and Jehoram. They had escorted the Levites to the festival and now stood in closed ranks in front of the advancing line of people who marched on the palace.

Behind them Jehoiada followed with a small group of Zealot Priests who had travelled from Samaria to witness the new King's anointing.

Jehoiada slowed as movement caught his eye. The fabric was expensive, too expensive to belong to anyone but Thaliah.

'Soldiers! To me!' Jehoiada called, knowing one of the commanders would heed his order.

He followed the deep blue silk which was vanishing around the corner of a narrow alley. He frowned wondering where she was going. He risked a glance behind him, smiling as he saw a few of the Zealot Priests and at least ten soldiers had answered his command.

'What are we doing?' one zealot asked as the High Priest slowed to peer cautiously around the next corner.

'Shush!' The man balked, clearly not accustomed to being told what to do.

Jehoiada moved on, signalling for everyone in tow to follow him. They reached the outside of Sheba's home and the Priest frowned, concern rising rapidly to create a knot in his chest. *Had the Princess betrayed him?*

****

Joash grabbed handfuls of the cold roast meat, yoghurt and salad and began shovelling them in his mouth like he had not eaten for a week. Aron and Sheba laughed aloud at his appetite.

'You cannot take the boy out of the King it seems.' Aron wrapped his arm around Sheba and hugged her to his chest.

The door burst open and Aron reached for his sword, realising he had taken it off as he entered Sheba's home. He peered down the hallway to see two palace guards, with Thaliah close behind, making their way to the back of the house.

'Sheba! Where are you?' The Queen entered the cookroom moments after her guards and stood with her hands on her hips, staring with unmasked annoyance at her step-daughter.

She smiled as the Princess's eyes darted to the boy, with thick curly black hair ringed by a golden circlet. His back was to her, but he spun around at the sound of her voice.

She watched as Sheba's bodyguard leant over the table, taking the boy by the shoulders and lifting him over the table in one fluid motion. He placed the boy between himself and the Princess protectively.

'Get him out of here Sheba.' The Princess grabbed Joash by the back of his collar as he grunted in protest. She dragged him as she backed out of the cookroom toward her own bedroom at the rear.

Aron looked at his sword, still in its scabbard, on the bench by the door through which the Queen had just entered.

'Are you looking for this?' Thaliah picked up the sword as her men drew their own.

Sheba felt for the doorknob at her back and opened her bedroom door. She pushed Joash into the room, pulling the door half closed between herself and her nephew. She quickly scanned the cookroom, hoping to help Aron.

The knife she had used moments earlier, still sat on the chopping block. It was right behind Aron, but he had not remembered it. As she opened the door to her room once more and stepped through, she called to him.

He turned, grabbed the knife and moved in front of her bedroom door. She could hear voices on the other side, but was frantically looking for an escape. Her window was small, but it was large enough for Joash to get through.

As the sound of blade on blade reached her, she pushed the window open and lifted Joash up as high as she could. 'Go to the temple Joash. Do not wait for me! Do not look back! Do you understand?' The boy nodded. She gave him a quick push as the door to her room exploded.

All she could think about was Aron as Thaliah stepped through.

'How in the world did you get him out of the palace?' The Queen did not expect an answer. 'You scheming little whore.' She stepped forward, both guards stood in the doorway behind her, and slapped the Princess across the face with the back of her hand.

Sheba did not flinch. She stood her ground and hit the Queen in return, not a back handed slap, but a full forced punch in the face. The woman staggered as the two guards could not decide if they should aid her or applaud.

'Sheba!' The Princess heard her husband's voice and for the first time in a long time was happy to have him in her house.

The guards turned, as the Queen realised she was cornered. She tried to move past Sheba, but the Princess grabbed her by the hair and pulled her to the ground.

The two guards dropped their swords as soon as they saw the cookroom filled with soldiers. Jehoiada rushed past them and into Sheba's room.

The Queen was still thrashing on the ground, with Sheba sitting on her back, the woman's hands pulled up behind her, keeping her in place.

'In here!' he called as two soldiers moved in. 'Take this, this harlot to the temple. I think a public execution is in order.'

'No! Jehoiada, please. We talked about this. Just imprison her.' The Princess begged her husband.

'I would rather die than rot away in prison.' The Queen puffed out her chest as two heavy-set soldiers pulled her to her feet by her arms.

'You heard the woman.' Jehoiada smiled.

Sheba pushed past her husband, her face pale. The Priest shrugged to himself until he followed Thaliah from the room, to find his wife, screaming at her bodyguard's side.

'Get some help.' The Princess tore a piece of fabric from her dress and scrunched it into a tight ball, she pressed it firmly to Aron's lower abdomen. 'Hurry!'

Jehoiada watched Sheba without helping or giving any order for anyone to move. 'What are you doing? Find a physician, now!' Sheba's eyes burrowed into him.

She returned her attention to Aron. 'No, no, no. Keep your eyes open Aron. Look at me.'

'Looks like we know where her loyalties lie,' Thaliah sneered. Jehoiada signalled for the guards to get her out, but did not leave the house.

'Sheba, come now. Leave him be. He is just a bodyguard. He was doing his job.' He put his hand on her shoulder, encouraging her to walk away.

She shrugged it away. 'If you do not get him some help, I swear you will regret it.' The Priest watched her expression. He had never seen her so angry. He had known the man loved his wife, but had never fully realised, until now, that she reciprocated his feelings.

He left the house, without another word.

Chapter 43

Joash hid inside the temple. The sun had dropped low in the sky and he was growing hungry, but he was too frightened to leave his hiding place.

He could hear the people returning to the temple courtyard. They sounded angry, or excited. It was hard to tell. Sheba had not come for him. Leah had not come for him. *Would anyone come for him?*

There were guards outside the room he was hiding in. He did not know if they were the Queen's guards, like the ones who came to his house.

Finally, he heard his uncle's voice. He sounded angry. He was calling to all the people in the courtyard. Joash could only hear the occasional word, like harlot, whore, depraved.

If his uncle was out there, then it must be safe, so he slowly wriggled out from inside the cupboard with all the priestly robes and crept from the room.

The two guards paid no attention to the boy as he slipped out to hide behind a pillar on the temple steps. It was dark now and only fire light shone from the many sconces that hung on the temple walls.

His uncle was standing next to a woman, who was on her knees. All around her, fires were alight, so that they both were easily visible. Their shadows cast eerie shadowy creatures all over the temple wall and Joash began to shiver with fear.

'I call each and every person who has been harassed, beaten, deprived of food, been used and abused by this woman to cast your stones.' Joash heard his uncle command and his shivering grew.

Were they really going to throws stones at this woman?

A guard moved forward first, a wide grin on his face. 'I will go first. I have endured this woman's foul temper and insults for seven years.' The Captain of the guard stepped up and threw a large rock at Thaliah.

She flinched but did now cry out. 'Next!' called the High Priest.

A line of people fanned out before the temple as the Priest stepped away from the bound woman.

Shouts sounded from too many voices for Joash to comprehend. He peered around the pillar, not being able to stop himself. The stones did not all find their mark, but many did. The

woman on her knees, was soon curled into a
ball on the ground, trying to hide her face, her
head, her legs, every part of her.

****

'I have seen enough.' Isaac moved away
from the roaring crowd. Leah followed.

'That was gruesome. I am so glad Sheba
and Aron took Joash away from that.'

'We had best check on them before we
leave.'

'Leave, so soon?' Leah held Isaac's hand
as they walked quickly from the temple through
the alleyways that led to the marketplace and
surrounding homes.

'The smell of death is disturbing me.'
Isaac grinned at the irony. Leah knew of his
past profession. He did not realise how much he
had missed the simple life of taking a contract
and killing someone, who usually deserved it,
for a nice fat pouch of coin.

As they approached the house, Isaac
began to run. The front door was broken in and
there were no lights on inside. A chill ran down
his spine as he entered the darkened hallway.
He reached the cookroom to find two Queen's
guard dead on the floor, flies buzzing around
their bodies even in the darkness.

'Aron! Sheba!' He moved toward
Sheba's room at the rear of the building. A soft

314

glow gave him hope that someone was there. As he entered the bedroom, he saw the Princess, her face lying on the pale form of his brother.

'No! Sheba, what happened?' Both he and Leah rushed to the Princess's side. She was groggy with unwelcomed sleep and struggled to open her eyes.

'What?' She, let Aron's hand go and rubbed her eyes. 'I did what I could.' Her tear-streaked face was barely visible in the dim candlelight. 'I dragged him in here, but I dared not leave to get a physician and I begged Jehoiada to send one, but one never came.'

Leah began lighting more candles and found an oil lamp, turning up the wick to cast more light into the room.

'Is he?' she asked as she peered over her friend's head.

'Not yet!' Sheba sobbed.

****

'We must do something.' Anath paced in mid-air. If the situation were not so serious, the scene would have been comical.

'We are forbidden.' Asherah barely held back her own tears.

'Surely we can find a physician to help them,' Anath continued, scrunching her nose in thought.

'She has help now. Hopefully Isaac will find the right person to aid his brother.' The Goddess watched as the faint light of Aron's spirit tugged back and forth between life and death.

'The boy King. He has seen much. We must send him help.' Astarte interrupted the scene they saw below.

'I will go to him.' Asherah shimmered and disappeared.

Moments later, she reached out of the veil and touched the boy's head with her hand. He opened his eyes, fighting to remain calm at the sight of what must have appeared to be a ghost to the small boy.

'You are safe Joash. Your Aunt sent me.' She spoke words into his mind and a wave of peace washed over him. 'Here, follow me.' The Priestess took the boy's hand and guided him through the darkness to his home.

Chapter 44

The streets were alive with celebrations as Isaac pushed his way into the dimly lit tavern. He found the physician well into his third ale and paid his bar tab to convince the man that his friend needed his help now, not tomorrow morning.

'Leah, get the physician some food. We need to sober him up a little.' Isaac pushed the man through the doorway into Sheba's room.

'My bag. I need my bag.' Isaac handed the swaying man a leather satchel which he began to rummage through, seemingly from memory.

He pulled out a handful of bottles and slowly made his way to Aron's bedside. Sheba moved away from him as a noise made them all turn toward the front door.

Isaac drew his sword and pushed the Princess behind him. Slowly he left her room and moved through the cookroom, toward the hallway. As he reached the end of the passage, he saw Joash. His face was ash white and he looked as though he could barely walk.

Isaac returned his sword to the scabbard and reached for the boy King just as he collapsed.

He carried Joash into the back room, a bewildered look on his face. 'Looks like we have another patient.' Leah jumped to her feet and made room on the smaller cot, where Joash usually slept.

'Bring him over here.' She searched his body for any wounds and finding none, touched his forehead with her cheek. 'He is not running a fever and there are no wounds.'

'Then stay with Aron.' Isaac pointed the physician back to his ever-paling brother.

'What are you doing?' Sheba asked as the man began tearing what was left of Aron's shirt off.

'This filth has to go or he will die of an infection. He has lost a lot of blood.' He opened the wound with his fingers and Sheba dry-reached but composed herself quickly.

'The wound has not festered yet.' Isaac stated from over the physician's shoulder. 'I have seen plenty of them in my time.'

'I bet you have.' The physician was slowly regaining his senses. He took a mouthful of the broth offered by Leah, his hands still occupied in Aron's stomach. 'He has a tear in his gut. I need to sew it.'

'I will help. Sheba, you go sit with Joash.' Isaac nodded to the boy as he sat down next to Aron on the bed. The Princess made to protest, but as the physician cut a larger hole in her lover's wound, she decided to move, quickly before the smell of beef broth and blood made her empty her stomach.

'What happened to Joash?' Leah whispered as she stroked the boy's brow.

'When we were attacked. I told him to go to the temple and hide. Then Jehoiada came and took the Queen to the temple to execute her.' The Princess held back the tears that were so close to bursting forth.

'You might need to slow down.' Leah patted her friend on the hand. 'Who attacked you?'

'Sorry. Thaliah stormed in with two guards. She took one look at Joash with his crown still on his head and realised it was her grandson. Her men attacked us, but thank Yahweh, Jehoiada was not far behind her. I am still unsure how he knew she was on her way here, but he arrived as I pushed Joash out the bedroom window and sent him to the temple to keep him safe.'

The Princess took a deep breath, trying to put the pieces together in her mind. Leah patted her hand and waited patiently, trying to drown

out the sound of cutting flesh and now searing
flesh behind them.

'Then I realised Aron was hurt. Jehoiada
would not send for help. He looked at me with
such disgust. I think he knows.'

'I have sewn the hole and burnt the
surface flesh to stop the bleeding. Here,' the
physician handed Isaac a mixture in a bowl.
'this is a salve, with nettle oil and Philistine
oak. Fill the wound daily and change the
dressing.'

'Will he be alright?' Sheba jumped to her
feet as the man moved to the door.

He shrugged. 'Only time will tell.' He
saw Joash asleep on the cot and frowned,
recognising the young King. 'Do you want me
to check on him?'

Sheba swung around, suddenly realising
she had not taken Joash's crown from his head.
'Yes. Please do.'

The physician moved in and lowered his
head to the boy's chest. He felt his forehead and
checked him over, pulling on the skin on the
back of his hands gently.

'He is exhausted and dehydrated. Take a
cloth soaked in fresh water and drop it to his
lips regularly.' He turned to leave, then
suddenly realised something. 'You should do

the same for him. He has lost a lot of blood and only water can help him replenish it.'

Leah and Sheba both jumped to their feet at once, almost knocking each other over. They collected two bowls and Leah cared for Joash, while Sheba did the same for Aron.

Isaac showed the physician out and dropped a coin in his hand. 'I owe you man. Any favour, just ask it.' The physician nodded, not realising exactly what Isaac was offering.

The assassin smiled to himself as he began walking to the back room once more. Just as he reached the doorway, he heard a sound from behind him.

'Have you seen Joash?' Jehoiada stood with his hands on his hips. 'I have too much work to arrange for tomorrow to be running all over town looking for that boy.'

Sheba heard the Priest speaking and moved to the door. 'How dare you.' Isaac placed his hand gently on Sheba's chest, hoping to stop her from what he knew she would regret.

'What?'

'You executed the Queen while Joash hid at the temple. He likely saw everything. He stumbled his way back here alone, afraid and barely conscious. On top of that, you left Aron to die. I told you I would never forgive you. Now get out.'

'Not without the King.'

'Yes, without the King.' Jehoiada opened his mouth to speak again, but Isaac turned to face the man, whose lips moved soundlessly at the assassin's look.

'I will return tomorrow with the King's guard. Have him ready to go.'

'Go where?'

'To the Baal temple. We have unfinished business to attend to, now that Thaliah is dead.

Chapter 45

Sheba could not stop pacing the floor of her room. Leah and Isaac had described the execution and even having not seen it, she was scarred by it.

Joash had awoken, thankfully with no memory of the previous night, but it was evident that Jehoiada fully intended to make sure Joash did not miss the next massacre.

'How can we stop him?'

'Who? Jehoiada?' Isaac asked, knowing full well who the Princess meant.

The Princess suddenly swung around, collected her robe and left the room. 'Watch Aron for me. I will be back before dawn,' she shouted as she made her way down the passageway. 'And find a new door!' she yelled over her shoulder as she pushed past the broken shards.

The Princess used what little moonlight there was to find her way to the grove of oaks just outside the walls. It was quiet on the streets now, with most revellers having found their way to their beds.

As soon as she found an empty patch of grass, the Princess dropped to her knees and clenched her hands in front of her chest.

'I would ask Yahweh, but I know you will answer Asherah.' Sheba waited. Her mind was thinking of the Goddess.

Asherah appeared transparent, floating before the Princess. The grove of oaks suddenly seemed lighter than before.

'It has been a long night.' Asherah's hair streamed behind her as though a strong wind blew, but the oaks did not even rustle.

'That is an understatement. Jehoiada plans to kill all the Baal priests and burn the temple tomorrow.' Asherah lowered herself to the ground and her appearance changed to a more substantial form.

'I know.' She knelt next to Sheba, her presence causing the hairs on the Princess's arm to stand on end.

'Then you must stop him. Too many innocent people will die. Many who worship there are not bad, they just follow the teachings of their ancestors instead of mine.'

The Goddess laughed. 'Well actually some of your ancestors worshipped Baal too, if you recall.'

'Yes, of course. What I mean.' The Goddess cut her off.

'I know what you mean. But I cannot interfere. It is forbidden to attack a human. How do you propose I stop him?'

'He is going to forcibly drag Joash out to watch. Like a rite of passage to becoming the most vicious king Judah has ever know.'

'I believe Joash will know better, in time.'

'But that will not save the hundreds of Priests and worshippers of Baal tomorrow.'

'No, it will not. I am sorry Princess.'

'Sorry. What kind of god allows his Priests to commit the very same atrocities his people have been subjected to? I do not understand.'

'I know you are angry.' Asherah touched the Princess's shoulder and a sense of calm flowed over her. 'You must learn that there are some things, many things, that you cannot change or repair.'

A single tear rolled down the Princess's face. 'Aron. Will he live? I would rather die trying to save the Baal priests than live another day without him.' Streams of tears began to run down her face and drop from her chin.

The Goddess wrapped her arm around the Princess and this time, she did not take the pain away. She allowed it to wash over the woman as her body shook with sobs.

Sometimes grief needed to be released, not subdued.

The Princess felt exhausted once the tears finally stopped, but she felt the burden was lighter than it had been in years.

'Thank you. How is it that Joash does not remember the Queen's execution?'

The Goddess smiled. 'He was lost. I just led him home. Now it is time for you to go home.'

Sheba nodded and stood to leave. She took a few steps then turned to ask a question, but the Goddess was gone. The silver sliver of moonlight was all that cast any glow on the grove of old oak trees.

****

'Are you sure we cannot help?' Astarte asked as Asherah returned through the veil.

'How? Baal has left his own temple, preferring to hide while the carnage takes place. Moloch is not involved. Of that I am sure. He likely still does not know Joash lives. This is humanity attacking their own. There is nothing we can do.'

'How can Father love them so much?' Anath sat down on a rock, next to a large pond that filled from the waterfall above.

'I really wish I could answer that question sister.' Asherah sat on another rock and looked up at the waterfall. It never ended, falling from nothingness above. The Goddess watched that nothingness, waiting, expecting, hoping against all hope that her Father would answer their question.

A shadow appeared above the three Goddesses as they sat amongst the flowers that carpeted the ground around the waterfall.

'Gabriel.' They all spoke in unison. The Archangel smiled as he landed softly in the deep grass, folding his wings away like they never existed.

'It is I.' He bowed. 'You all look troubled.'

'We are. Very troubled.' Anath pouted and Astarte threw a pebble at her.

'This is serious.' Anath only pouted again.

'What is serious?' The Archangel sat cross-legged on the grass, his head still level with the Goddesses even upon their rocks.

'The new King is anointed.' Asherah started.

'That is good news.'

'It is, but there is death to follow tomorrow and the poor young boy will witness it all.'

Gabriel scrunched his nose as he considered how to respond. 'It is true. Many of the Baal priests will die tomorrow. Some have truly committed great evil, but many have not.'

'Do we not fight to bring the Redeemer of all humanity to pass so that *all* can be forgiven?' Asherah interrupted, her frustration rising. Gabriel put up his hand defensively.

'Let me finish. Yes, the Redeemer will ensure they are forgiven their dark deeds. He will take the burden of their sins, but still there will be those who do not see eternity as reward enough.'

'Who would not want eternity?' Asherah frowned, turning to her sisters for confirmation of the insanity of such a statement. Both nodded they agreed.

'It is easy for you to understand Asherah. You already live forever. Only the fallen can truly die. But humans, they live such short lives in this realm. They measure things in days. Take your Princess for instance. She still considers if she should stay or go. She still believes she can make a difference. Most of humanity does not think as she does. They think only of tomorrow.

You asked why Father loves them so? It is because of people like her, people willing to sacrifice everything for someone else or a cause greater than themselves.'

'But the Priest does the same thing. He is a Zealot, intent on destroying the Baal temple and all the Baal priests in Father's name.' Asherah could hear her own argument in her ears as she spoke. She knew the answer before it left Gabriel's lips.

'I see,' she said aloud.

'See what?' Anath protested.

'Do you want me to explain, or will you?' Gabriel asked, his eyes dark and gentle.

'The Priest is no different from Sheba. He is passionate about what he is doing. He is doing it for the greater good and willing to sacrifice much to see it come to pass. That is why Father loves them so.'

Astarte looked at Anath and shrugged. 'I am a warrior, not a philosopher. You lost me at the Priest not being different from the Princess. He has forced a boy to become a king before his time. He has put his ambition before his wife and her nephew and he has killed in cold blood.'

'Yes, but he fights the ambition. He focusses on the cause—to bring Yahweh's temple back to prominence in the culture of Israel. He believes the deaths are justified.' Gabriel explained as Anath scoffed.

'You sound like Moloch,' she goaded. 'That is his way of thinking.'

'That is why Father loves him too. That is why even Dagon was given a place with Father after all the terrible things he did. If even the Fallen can be redeemed, why not the worst of humanity?' Gabriel stood to leave.

'I agree about redemption Gabriel.' Asherah also stood. 'But if what you say is true and all will be redeemed and I believe they will, then why should all of humanity not just do whatever they want, when they want? Why should Sheba stay and care for the King? Why should she not leave her husband and run away with Aron?'

'There is no reason why she should not. Father would think no less of her. It is how she sees herself now, in this realm, in this time that matters.' Gabriel opened his wings and launched himself into the waterfall mist above.

The sisters remained silent for quite some time, all deep in their own thoughts. Finally, Anath spoke, rolling her eyes. 'Well that was helpful.' The three Goddesses laughed softly.

As they took flight, Asherah pondered the Archangel's words. There was only one good thing left to come from all of this. She descended through the veil and gasped at the scene below.

Chapter 46

There had been no stopping Jehoiada. As promised, dawn brought a personal guard of ten soldiers to escort the new King to his palace. Sheba had promised she would join him as soon as she could, but as he left her home, she saw the fear in his eyes.

'He is only seven Jehoiada,' she called after the Priest. 'Seven.'

There was no reply, just the quiet sobs of Leah. A groan brought the Princess from her brooding. She ran back to her bedroom to find Aron struggling to rise.

'Stay where you are. You cannot move yet. The physician said so.' She rushed to his side and pushed him gently back onto the bed. 'Leah,' the Princess called out but Leah was already moving through the door with a bowl full of broth.

Sheba began spooning small portions into Aron's mouth. He tried to speak, but she was having none of it. Each time he opened his mouth, she placed another spoonful in.

Finally, Aron lifted his hand to hers and stopped her from placing another spoonful in his mouth. 'Stop woman.' He smiled to soften the words.

His lips cracked with the smile and he winced, but Sheba did not care. She kissed him firmly and began spooning food once more. 'Food, then questions. You scared me half to death,' she scolded.

Aron winked at his brother who stood leaning against the doorway. 'You delayed our leaving you know,' he chided good-naturedly.

Aron shrugged. 'It was not on purpose. I promise you. Where is Joash?'

'He is safe,' Sheba answered before putting the final spoonful into Aron's mouth.

'That is good, but where is he?'

'With Jehoiada. I could not stop them from taking him. They brought ten guards this morning and took him away.'

'They?'

'Jehoiada really, just Jehoiada. He is obsessed.'

'I need to go to Joash.' Aron tried to move, but winced.

'No, you cannot.' Isaac interrupted. 'There is nothing you can do brother. He is the King now; anointed, accepted by the Levites, the Priest, the people.'

'I will go to him as soon as you are on your feet once more.' Sheba promised.

'You are not going to stay?' Isaac asked, shaking his head incredulously.

'I am.' Sheba stood to take the bowl from the room, but Leah interrupted.

'Why?' she asked.

'Because it is my duty. He is my nephew, my blood. I need to look after him.'

'You said yourself that Jehoiada likely knows about you and Aron. That might not be safe,' her friend protested.

'Safe or not. I must try. Jehoiada is not going to be soft on Joash now he is King. The child needs some love in his life.'

'Let her be.' Aron interrupted. 'Go to him now Sheba. I am fine.'

Sheba looked to Leah who nodded she would watch over Aron.

The Princess pulled her robe on and walked to the doorway. She stopped and looked back at Aron, his face still pale. 'Drink lots of water, and more broth.' He smiled as she turned and left.

Isaac looked at Aron and nodded at the pleading look in the man's eyes. 'I will follow her. I cannot promise the Priest will not die, but she will be safe. You have my word.'

****

The Princess did not reach the palace before the mounted riders rode past her. At the rear, the King's chariot rode proudly with Jehoiada at the reins and Joash barely able to see over the front.

She tried to be heard above the sound of horses' hooves on cobbled stone streets, but it was useless. The boy did not see her. He was riding to watch death and she would not be there for him.

Isaac moved up behind her and she jumped as he tapped her on the shoulder. 'It seems you are too late. Shall we go home? You can return tomorrow, after all this is over and console the boy.'

'No. I need to try and stop this before it gets out of hand.'

'How?' Isaac opened his hands palms up. 'It will be over before we reach the temple.'

'Damn it.' She stomped as the words the Goddess spoke came to her. *You must learn that there are some things, many things, that you cannot change or repair.*

Isaac took her by the shoulders and steered her away from the main thoroughfare, back to the alley. The last thing he needed was for someone to recognise her. Now that Joash was King, she was Aunt to the King.

****

Joash watched Mattan, the Baal priest as he was dragged outside the temple.

'What is your verdict your Grace?' Jehoiada bowed as he waited for the boy to give the order.

They had rehearsed these events all the way back from Sheba's house to the palace and Joash had recited the words like an actor in a play.

In his mind, he decided that was what he was doing. He was like the performers he had seen in the marketplace on the Sabbath. They wore make up and dressed in fancy clothes and retold the stories of past glories, where Kings of Judah and Israel had died fighting the evil of other nations or religions.

'He has committed sins against Yahweh. He must die.' Jehoiada nodded his approval.

'You heard your king. The sentence is death. Mattan, you are found guilty of sins against the house of Yahweh.' The Priest blinked as though he had just woken from a bad dream.

A long spear struck the man in the chest, and he gasped, before falling to his knees, holding the shaft like a deadly adder. Joash turned away, but Jehoiada forced him to look.

'This is what happens to those who oppose the one true God. Yahweh has delivered us a true born heir of King David. He has delivered enemies into our hands.'

Joash closed his eyes as Mattan began to choke on the blood spilling from his lips. He tried to speak but the words would not pass his lips. His eyes rolled back as he toppled sideways and thrashed. The movement stopped quickly, but Joash kept his eyes closed.

'Fire the temple.' Jehoiada ordered and soldiers lit torches from the previous night's still burning coals. They rode around the temple, casting fiery branches into any window or doorway they could find.

People began to spill from the temple, but they were struck down with arrows or spears.

'Uncle?' Joash tugged on the Priest's robe.

'What my King.' He bowed reverently.

'Why are we killing them all?'

'Because they worship Baal.'

Joash nodded understanding he did not have, as the screams began to drift from the burning temple.

Chapter 47

Sheba walked the perimeter of the temple ruins and sighed. Isaac watched like an eagle, wondering what she was thinking. He did not envy his brother. She was more than a handful.

'I need to go to the palace, now.' Sheba started walking toward the place that was once her home. So many memories flooded her mind… Ahaziah, her father, but she pushed them aside. 'You do not need to come. I doubt anyone is going to harm the King's aunt.'

Isaac shrugged and followed.

'You are quiet today.' the Princess said once she realised he was coming with her.

'I am just wondering what you are thinking.'

'I am thinking I will have to stay with Joash and help him understand all this.' She cast her arm around her as they moved past the last of the carnage. The smell of burnt flesh still hung in the air and the guards had not even bothered to bury the dead.

'How can you help him understand something like this when you can barely comprehend it yourself?'

'I have to try.'

'Why? Because he is your nephew? What chance do you have against his regent; the man appointed by the temple to guide the new King; the man backed by Jehu and his Zealot fanatics?'

'You think I should leave?' Sheba stopped, her hands on her hips defensively.

'I think you have done all you can. I am also concerned your husband may decide to have you stoned for your relationship with Aron.'

'Even if he knows, Joash will not agree to do anything to hurt me.'

'Jehoiada is his regent. If he deems the King is compromised, he will overrule him. You know he can.'

Sheba tried not to think about such an idea. 'I believe he is not that shallow.' Surely Jehoiada would not be so vindictive?

'I hope you are right.' Isaac's tone spoke volumes, but Sheba turned and carried on.

When they reached the palace, they were offered a cool drink while they waited in the courtyard. They had barely taken a seat when a guard ushered them through for an audience with the King.

As the Princess entered the throne room, she felt a chill at what she saw. Her husband,

Jehoiada sat upon her stepmother's old throne and her nephew was nowhere in sight.

'Sheba,' the Priest smiled, but it failed to reach his eyes. 'Where is your usual *bodyguard*?'

'Not shallow at all.' Isaac whispered before stepping back to guard the Princess.

'He is recovering, no thanks to you.'

'Be careful Princess.' Jehoiada warned.

'Where is Joash?'

'He was very tired from this morning's endeavours. He has taken an afternoon rest.'

'Then I will return when he is able to see me. I am his aunt. I simply wish to offer him my aid, should he require it.'

'You are not needed in the palace *wife*. Return to your *home*.'

'I am Joash's aunt. He lives because I, and my *bodyguard* and *his* brother saved his life, while you prayed in the temple.' Isaac moved forward. He could see this was not going to end well.

'Time to leave Princess.' He refrained from touching her, but only just.

'I want to see my nephew,' Sheba demanded.

'Leave now, or I will publicly call for your death and that of your *bodyguard*. Do you understand me Sheba?'

'What happened to you?' Isaac was pulling on the Princess's arm now, but she was not moving. The Priest's face went pale as he looked his wife squarely in the eyes.

'Take her.' Jehoiada demanded to the guards. 'Arrest her for adultery. And you!' The new regent pointed at Isaac who had reached for his sword before remembering he had been asked to relinquish it before he came in. 'You, tell your brother we are coming for him.'

Sheba struggled to free herself as Isaac watched her, deciding what he should do. 'Get to Aron, save Aron.' She drew a sword from the guard's belt and stepped back, ready to defend herself.

Isaac left the throne room, taking no chances. He knew Sheba was giving him the time he needed. Jehoiada would not kill her in the throne room. He would want a public execution.

****

Sheba sat in the dungeon, wondering when Jehoiada had become the man he was today.

The dungeon doors opened and Joash ran to the bars, reaching for his aunt who took his hand. He took a deep breath and put on a brave face before turning to his uncle who followed him in.

'You will have her released at once.' Sheba almost cried at the sound of his little defiant voice.

'I am sorry your Grace but she has embarrassed you and me.'

'What are you talking about?' the little boy was returning.

'Your aunt has been having an affair with Aron.' Jehoiada explained as if Joash were a simpleton.

'I know.' Joash scowled. 'I am not embarrassed, now let her go.'

'She must be made an example of.'

'This has nothing to do with embarrassment to the throne, this is about your own shame Jehoiada. My brother promised you my hand on three conditions. Do you recall what they were?'

Jehoiada did not answer. He only glared at his wife and gently steered the King from the dungeon.

'I do.' Sheba screamed after him. 'You were to make me happy and do whatever that took. You were to protect Joash and you were to ignore his mother. You have failed at all three. You want to kill me to kill your shame.'

Chapter 48

Sheba brought her bound hands to her eyes to cover them from the sun. Two days had passed and she had not seen daylight. Her clothing was torn and she knew her face was covered in dirt and grime.

Rough hands forced her into a caged wagon as she tried to gain some sense of where she was. This was a part of the palace she had never seen before.

'A shame the King said we cannot molest this one.' A guard with a blackened front tooth and no neck pinched her backside before he closed the gate.

The ride was short as the cart pulled up outside the palace gates on the promenade that led to the temple. A makeshift stage had been erected just for the occasion.

'The temple steps too good for my stoning?' the Princess remarked as the same guard pulled her from the wagon. 'I would have thought the High Priest would have at least done me the same honour as my step-mother,' Sheba goaded the guards.

She was bound, but not useless. If she could draw one of their weapons, they would be forced to kill her before the stoning. Then she would know peace.

Her only consolation was that she was alone. Isaac must have reached Aron in time. She could die a happy woman.

'What are you smiling about?' The sound came from a shadow cast by the sun at his back, but the voice was unmistakable.

'You did not get Aron. At least the man who saved the King still lives.'

Jehoiada moved closer and dragged the Princess up onto the stage. 'I loved you once.'

'I respected you once,' the Princess retorted. 'But then you made a little boy watch a massacre and now, I am guessing you are going to have him watch my death.'

The Priest paled. 'You left me no choice. I told you to leave Joash to me. Your family has tainted the King's line with talk of tolerance and equality for generations. It stops now.'

'You really believe Yahweh needs you to restore his temple to greatness? You are a little human. I have seen the divinity you crave to see. You do it no honour.'

Jehoiada pushed Sheba forward as two guards pulled her to her knees. The priest began to speak, but the Princess chose not to listen to his pompous lies. Instead, she scanned the faces in the crowd below. A face smiled back at her that she recognised, but she thought she had lost her mind from days of hunger.

As Jehoiada called for the first person to cast the first stone a hooded figure moved forward. He walked with a limp and juggled a large rock from one hand to the other.

'Well, throw the stone then.' Jehoiada stepped back as the man drew back his arm and his hood in one motion. The rock left his hand, as Jehoiada suddenly recognised the wielder, but it was too late. The rock struck the Priest in the forehead and as he crumpled to the ground, a wall of gravel began to rise from the ground like a desert sandstorm.

The sound of horses could be heard as men bellowed orders at one another. The gravel grew thicker, forcing the crowd to begin seeking cover. Only a handful of guards milling about remained. They struggled to decide if they should join the crowd or seek to fight an unseen enemy.

Sheba looked at her husband, unconscious on the stage. The two guards who had forced her to her knees were gone and the Princess stood, peering through the gravel, trying to make out a figure moving toward her.

She found Aron's face through the spiralling wall of airborne gravel that whirled around her, leaving her entirely untouched.

Aron moved gingerly, but still managed to vault to the stage. He too moved in a void of air, surrounded by a funnel of gravel.

The sound of horses grew closer as Aron wrapped his arm around the Princess's waist. 'Jump when I say so.' She nodded, understanding in her eyes.

'Now!' Aron moved forward and she followed as two horsemen moved past them, slowing to a trot with two more horses trailing behind them.

An arrow shot past Sheba's head, but it was deflected by the whirling gravel. The horses had blinkers on to protect their eyes and they were remarkably calm as they waited for their riders to tell them what to do. The reins for both horses were thrown back and the four pushed their mounts into a gallop as soldiers' shouts became lost in the whirling debris.

****

Moloch moved alongside the Goddess as the wall of gravel fell to the ground. 'Interfering again sister.'

'No humans were harmed.'

'Not like last time you used that barrier.' The Goddess raised an eyebrow.'

'I thought you did not know.'

'I did not realise the boy was saved that night, but I heard about the gravel sandstorm that helped the Princess escape. Men died that night.'

'But I did not kill them.'

'You split hairs.'

Asherah shrugged. 'I have never taken a host. You took Mattan's body from him more than once.'

It was Moloch's turn to raise an eyebrow. 'Now what?'

'Now I make sure a king does not go mad at the hands of his uncle.'

Moloch nodded. 'The line continues then?'

'It does. You will not stop it Moloch. If, by some slim chance I do not see what you are doing, Father will. The Redeemer must come. If he does not, humanity will continue to fight over which religion is right and who is righteous enough to please Yahweh, while we will continue to lose ourselves over where we fit in Father's plan.'

Moloch shrugged. 'It is a long-life sister. What else is there if there is no conflict?' He smiled and disappeared.

'Peace, harmony, love.' The Goddess sighed.

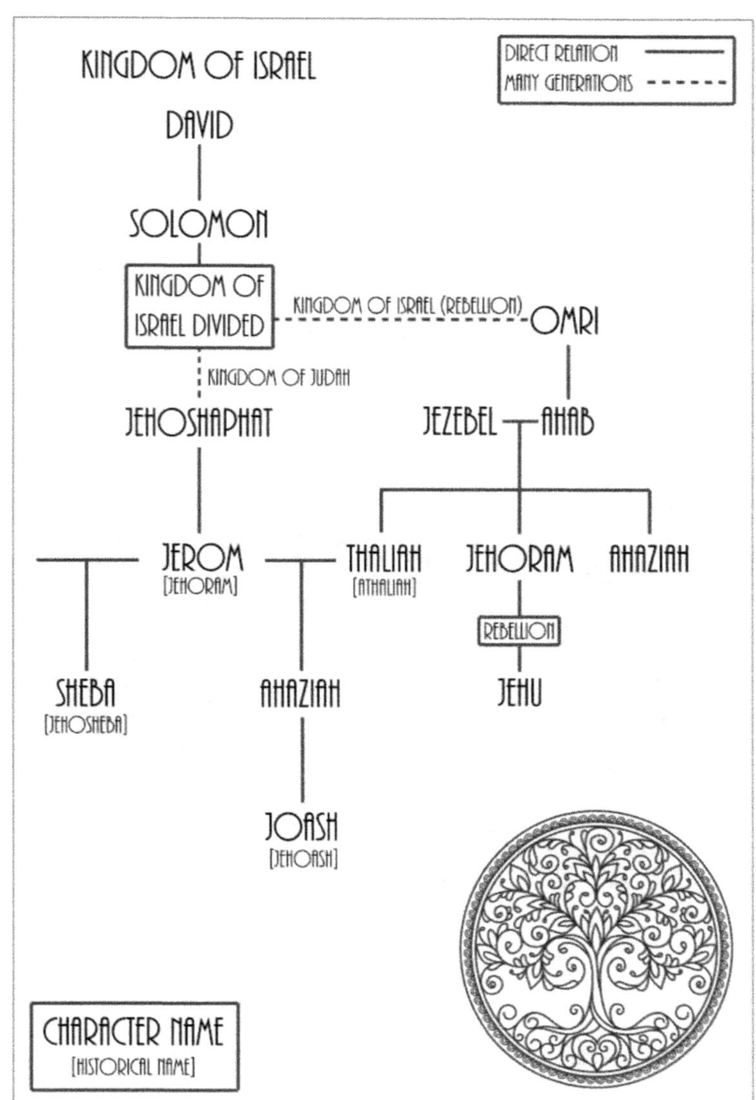

KINGDOM OF ISRAEL
DAVID
SOLOMON
KINGDOM OF ISRAEL DIVIDED
KINGDOM OF ISRAEL (REBELLION)
OMRI
KINGDOM OF JUDAH
JEHOSHAPHAT
JEZEBEL
AHAB
JEROM
[JEHORAM]
THALIAH
[ATHALIAH]
JEHORAM
AHAZIAH
REBELLION
SHEBA
[JEHOSHEBA]
AHAZIAH
JEHU
JOASH
[JEHOASH]
DIRECT RELATION
MANY GENERATIONS
CHARACTER NAME
[HISTORICAL NAME]

What Next!

Reign of Retribution is the final book in *The Eternal Realm* series. If you enjoyed it, why not go back and start from the beginning with my first series – *Covenant of Grace* – it is complete and you can start your journey with book 1– *Destiny of Kings* free. Just visit my website www.atime2write.com.au and sign up for my newsletter. I'll send you a free copy.

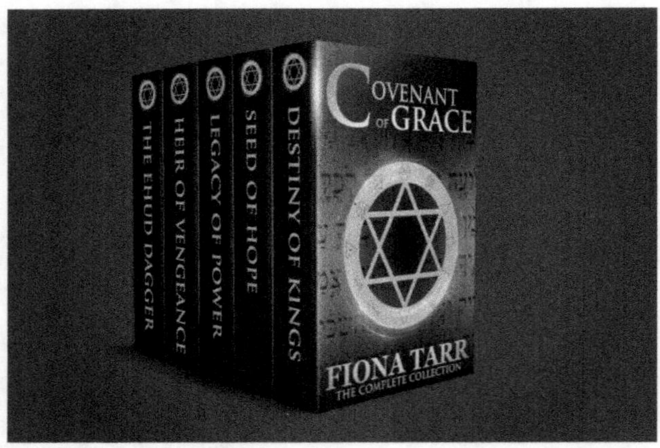

To find out more about my current work, you can follow me on Facebook, Instagram or find me on my website above.

Thanks again for reading.

Reviews!

I love to know what readers think of my books. If you have a moment, please check back with your ebook store or paperback retailer and share your review.

Reviews help me develop my writing, but most of all, they continue to encourage me to write more books and help others decide if my stories might be worth a read.

Books by Fiona Tarr

The Eternal Realm Series

Book 1 – The Jericho Prophecy
Book 2 – Delilah and the Dark God
Book 3 – Reign of Retribution
****

The Priestess Chronicles Series

Book 1 – Call of the Druids
Book 2 – Relic Seeker

****

The Covenant of Grace Series

Book 1 – Destiny of Kings
Book 2 – Seed of Hope
Book 3 – Legacy of Power
Book 4 – Heir of Vengeance
Prequel – The Ehud Dagger
Boxed Set – The Complete Collection
****